Only If
You Can
Find Me

Only If You Can Find Me

PATRICIA LAUREL

MUTUAL PUBLISHING

Library of Congress Cataloging-in-Publication Data

Laurel, Patricia.
  Only if you can find me / Patricia Laurel.
      p. cm.
  Summary: "A nine-year-old Filipino-American girl visits the Philippines and
discovers the special gift that saves her and her family from the spell of a vengeful
duwende and the schemes of an evil cousin"--Provided by publisher.
  ISBN-13: 978-1-56647-798-7 (softcover : alk. paper)
  ISBN-10: 1-56647-798-0 (softcover : alk. paper)
  1. Filipino American girls--Philippines--Fiction. 2. Dwarfs--Fiction. 3. Domestic
fiction. I. Title.
  PS3612.A944227O55 2006
  813'.6--dc22

                              2006020278

First Printing, September 2006
1 2 3 4 5 6 7 8 9

ISBN-10: 1-56647-798-0
ISBN-13: 978-1-56647-798-7

Book Design by Mardee Domingo Melton
Cover and interior illustrations by J. Orosa Paraiso

Mutual Publishing, LLC
1215 Center Street, Suite 210
Honolulu, Hawai'i 96816
Ph: (808) 732-1709
Fax: (808) 734-4094
e-mail: info@mutualpublishing.com
www.mutualpublishing.com

Printed in Taiwan

To Samantha,
Wherever you are

My sincere gratitude to my partner and best editor,
John Windrow, my mother and father, my siblings,
Sister Mary John Mananzan, Solo and Nani Mahoe,
Joel Paraiso, Ugu Bigyan, friends and relatives, and
the ghosts of my family's history who helped and
encouraged me.

Contents

Introduction

The little girl presses against the streaked bay window and watches the gray rain make puddles on Bush Street. She likes the sunny days in San Francisco the best, when the white clouds race across the sky toward the blue Pacific Ocean. But today is dreary. She is deep in thought and does not notice the man in white on the sofa behind her. He has a look of concern.

Her name is Samantha, but everyone calls her Sammy or Sam. Something has made her parents terribly upset. She hears them talking in the kitchen. She listens to her mother's frantic sobs while her father tries to calm her. Sammy is afraid. It's hard to know what to do when you're 9 years old.

"It's OK, Yvonne," her dad says to her mother. "It's going to be OK."

Sammy is trying to put it all together, all that happened over the past few weeks when her family flew across the Pacific Ocean to Hawai'i and the Philippines. She should have paid more attention to her inner voices.

I wish I had listened better to Lolo Ciano and Solo about being careful. Maybe this whole thing might never have happened and my mom and dad wouldn't be so scared now, she tells herself.

Sammy turns from the window and sees Lolo Ciano on the sofa. Her great-great-great uncle is invisible to others, but

Sammy can see him. She knows she can communicate with him with mind talk. She leaps to the sofa and hugs him.

I'm so glad to see you, Lolo Ciano! Where have you been? Are you here to help me? Oh please, please. I'm in so much trouble!

He holds up his hand.

Samantha, I know you have many questions, but it will take time to figure out what to do.

Sammy throws up her hands.

I have no words. I can't tell my parents anything! I try to write it down, but my writing turns to chicken scratch. They don't know what's happened.

Sammy has much to say to her uncle. Now her parents come into the living room, and they see their little girl gesturing wildly.

"She's doing it again!" Yvonne cries, the panic returning.

Jack looks worriedly at his daughter. He puts his hands on her shoulders and gently says, "Sweetie, your mother and I are getting really worried. Can you try and tell us what's going on?"

Sammy stares at him helplessly. The words won't come. Tears come instead. Jack leads Sammy to the sofa. Sammy is careful not to sit on Lolo Ciano.

The doorbell rings, and Jack goes to answer it.

Patricia Laurel

Mari and her daughter, Victoria, rush inside. Mari goes immediately to her sister, Yvonne. They hug each other and both start talking at once.

Victoria moves toward the couch and Lolo Ciano walks to the fireplace, making room for Sammy's cousin. Victoria quietly takes Sammy's hand. Usually Victoria is a chatterbox, but today is different. The two girls sit and listen to the grownups.

"We still have jet lag," Mari says. "It took all our energy to get dressed and drive over to the city."

"Did you call Mom and the others?" Yvonne asks, hugging her again, so distracted that she forgot the first hug.

"Yes. They're so worried they went to see a *manghuhula*."

Victoria whispers into Sammy's ear, "Mom says a *manghuhula* is a sooth sayer, kind of like a fortune teller."

"Have you been to the doctor?" Mari asks.

"Yes, and they ran all kinds of tests. They say there is nothing wrong. Sammy is as healthy as a little horse," Yvonne says.

They look despairingly at Sammy sitting on the couch.

"So what did the *manghuhula* say?" Yvonne asks Mari.

But before we get to what is ailing Sammy, we must back up a few weeks.

It all began when…

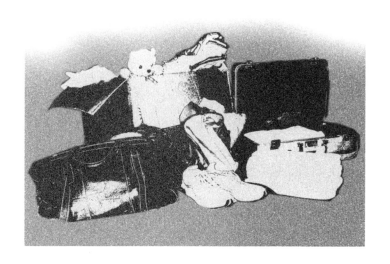

The Preparation

Not so long ago, there lived…

"SAMANTHA! Where are you?"

The girl's face pops up from the pages of her book. She is nine years old, with thick black hair, worn in bangs and braids. She is skinny with prominent features, high cheekbones and almond eyes like most of the women in her family. She has no baby fat. She is growing up now, with long arms and gangly legs.

Her Filipina grandmother, who Sammy calls Lola, says Sammy has pixie eyes — brown eyes with a warm glow. She has eyes like a fairy, Lola says. Lola is certain that Sammy has a gift, that she sees more than other people.

The brown eyes shine when Sammy is happy or excited.

Sammy knows from the tone of her mother's voice that she better get into the living room.

She lives in San Francisco, California, with her parents, Jack and Yvonne Plum, in a three-bedroom condo in an Edwardian house with a vast bay window looking out onto Pacific Heights and the city.

Jack can walk to his job at the bank on Van Ness Avenue. Yvonne never learned to drive, so she and Sammy go everywhere by bus, taxi, cable car, or on foot.

Sammy loves going about the city with her mother — window-shopping at the classy shops and boutiques on Union Street, winding through the crowded sidewalks of Chinatown where fish, lobsters and crabs in great glass tanks idly blow bubbles, and men with cleavers whack up dishes of crispy chicken or orange-roasted duck, or trudging up a hill and seeing the bright blue Pacific Ocean and the red Golden Gate Bridge soaring across the mouth of the white-capped bay.

Japan Center, with its pagoda that reminds her of a big Christmas tree, is only a few blocks from their house. The Plum family eats there often, because Jack and Yvonne are very fond of sushi. Sammy prefers tempura and chicken teriyaki.

Sammy loves books. She gets along well with her cousins, but is not nearly so chatty, antsy and busy as they are. She takes after her father, who is more reserved. While she can be happy at a swarming family gathering, she never dreads being alone. Give her a book to read and a dictionary to look up new words and she can be happy for hours.

"SAMANTHA PLUM!"

Sammy sighs, marks her page and runs to the living room, where she steps around and over the boxes her mother is packing. Clothes, house wares, food and other things are piled high. Yvonne, who is so meticulous that it drives Jack and Sammy to distraction, checks every item against her list. Yvonne thrives on detailed planning. If the house is one bit out of order, she is one bit out of sorts, and her exasperation grows bit by bit, until her house is in order again. She is out of sorts now — with all the hurly burly of getting ready for the big trip. Yvonne's four sisters tell her she would scrub and disinfect the whole planet if she had her way. Her five brothers agree.

Yvonne was just a child when the family left the Philippines. Her mother, Sammy's Lola, is a retired widow who spends half her time in California and the other half in her hometown of San Pablo, Philippines. Her sisters and brothers are spread all over — California, Canada, Hawai'i, Texas and Germany.

"Samantha, how do you expect me to finish all this packing when your things are everywhere? We're leaving tomorrow and I have a million things to do."

Sammy scampers about, getting toys and books out of her mother's way.

"You'll be sorry if your toys and books get packed with this other stuff. Some unfortunate child will be so thrilled to receive them," says Yvonne, bending down to put some carefully folded clothes in a box.

"Gather up your things, take them to your room and come back and help me, OK? I need to label everything so I'll know what's what when I distribute them."

Sammy nods dutifully, her arms filled with her belongings.

"When we've done that, maybe we can go down to Fillmore so I can buy some last-minute things," Yvonne says, her voice softening.

Sammy gets busy. When they are done, Yvonne says, "Why don't we go by Marie Jean's after we run our errands and treat ourselves to cream puffs?"

Sammy's eyes light up. Marie Jean has a bakery and coffee shop on Fillmore. She lives a few doors down the street from the Plums. Marie Jean creates the greatest pastries Sammy has ever tasted, but Number One on her list is the miniature, caramel-glazed creampuffs. She could eat them by the dozen.

After helping her mother fill many shopping bags, Sammy drinks in the heavenly, warm aromas of pastries and coffee as they open the jingling door of Marie Jean's bakery.

"*Bonjour*, neighbors!" The baker with her coiffed black hair and blue eyes pecks them on each cheek, leaving a faint red lipstick mark. "I thought you would come in today. 'Allo Sammee, I bet I know why you're here."

Sammy and Yvonne gratefully sit at a marble-top table and flop their bags on the floor. Sammy loves Marie Jean's musical accent.

She and her father often play the language game in the streets of the city, picking out Filipino, French, Italian, Japanese and Chinese.

Sammy remembers the time Tita Mari got really mad at Victoria for making fun of someone's accent. Sammy and Victoria were in a restaurant with their mothers. The Filipino waiter's name was Miguel. He was very courteous and chatted with Yvonne and Mari in Tagalog, the language of the everyday people in the Philippines.

He said something in English that none of them could understand.

"Would we like to see the what, Mom?" Victoria asked.

The waiter repeated the word a couple of times. Then Victoria blurted out, "Oh, you mean MENU, not minu!" She started to giggle. The waiter smiled, but Sammy saw the hurt in his eyes.

Mari's red face stopped Victoria's giggling immediately. "Apologize to Miguel," her mother said.

"I'm sorry, Miguel. I didn't mean to laugh at you," Victoria said, choking back her tears.

Mari said a few words in Tagalog to Miguel.

"It's all right, ma'am. All newcomers go through it," he replied.

He winked at Victoria, took everyone's orders and left.

Marie Jean comes to sit with them, carrying a plate of cream puffs warm from the oven, the caramelized topping moist and sticky.

"Almost, I forget," Marie Jean goes behind the counter and brings back a pastry box wrapped in pink ribbon. Sammy eyes the box hungrily even as she reaches for her second creampuff. "*Voila!* A little sweet treat to take home. You will share them with Papa, yes Sammee?"

Sammy listens to the adults chat, munching away. Yvonne notices the time.

"We have to run, Sammy. Your father will be home soon and I still have a bazillion things to do," Yvonne says, getting up from the table.

"I come and pick up the keys tomorrow, *Cherie*. Don't worry, I water your plants, feed your cat, bring in your mail." Marie Jean buzzes them again on each cheek.

Jack Plum is on the couch, listening to music when they return. He loves music, reading and solitude. He still gets rattled when his wife's huge family descends upon them. He likes to hide in his office when they visit, venturing out only for meals. But when he is drawn into a discussion, he can talk intelligently about nearly anything.

"You're home early, dinner isn't ready," Yvonne says, heading for the kitchen.

"I finished early and dumped the rest of the work on my assistant," Jack says, following his wife and daughter into the kitchen. "No office for three weeks. I can't wait to get to the farm where there are no phones. Just books. Bliss!"

Yvonne shoos them out of the kitchen. "You two do something useful, while I whip up dinner," she says.

Later, Sammy helps Yvonne clear the table and put the dishes in the dishwasher. Jack flops into his favorite chair and picks up the newspaper.

"Dad, are you all packed?" Sammy asks, running into the living room.

Jack winks at her. "I leave all that to your mother. She won't let me pack, I'm not organized enough."

Yvonne ignores his remarks and says, "Do you realize this is the first time in 20 years the entire family will be together in one place? Can you imagine?

Jack groans softly.

"Maybe the guys and I can plan a few excursions ourselves. The members of the sisterhood will stick to each other like glue, afraid to miss out on some family gossip. Like you don't all yak on the phone enough already."

Yvonne oozes mock compassion. "Poor thing. Can't handle the big family scene." She gives him a poor baby pat on the head.

Jack makes some more grumbling noises and puts his face behind his newspaper.

"Are Tita Patti and Tito John getting on the plane when we stop over in Honolulu?" Sammy asks. Yvonne's sister Patti and her husband, John live in Honolulu, on the island of O'ahu.

"Yes, Sweetie. Now help me finish with these boxes," Yvonne says.

Sammy checks her list one last time:

Sammy's List

Toothbrush	*Tales of Narnia*
Hairbrush	*Pocket Dictionary*
Pens/Pencils	*Starburst*
Snuggles	*Oreo Cookies*
GummiBears	*Sandals*
Sneakers	*Pick-Up Sticks*
Cards	*Cheeze-It Crackers*
Journal	*Travel Pillow*
Beef Jerky	*Lola's present*

After she finishes checking her list, Sammy gets herself ready for bed, thinking about what an adventure her big trip will be.

2

The Dream

The journey begins…

Sammy is so excited thinking about her first big trip away from home that she cannot sleep. Her head is full of imagined wonders about the trip across the Pacific Ocean to the islands of the Philippines. She turns to one of her books, which nearly always does the trick, but not tonight. Finally after tossing about, she turns off the night-light and screws her eyes shut, willing herself to sleep, thinking about the Tagalog song, "Bahay Kubo," that Lola taught her. She sings softly to herself.

Bahay Kubo, kahit munti, ang halaman doon ay sari-sari

Singkamas at Talong, Sigadilyas at Mani

Sitaw, Bataw, Patani

Kundol, Patola, Upa't Kalabasa

at saka mayroon pang Labanos, Mustasa

Sibuyas, Kamatis, Bawang at Luya

Da Da Da Da Da Da

That's all she can remember, so she adds the Da, Da, Da. She makes a mental note to ask Lola to teach her the rest of the song.

PATRICIA LAUREL

The song is about a hut. Although it is very small, it has a splendid garden — turnips, eggplants, string beans, squash, onion, garlic and tropical vegetables unknown to Sammy.

She turns this way and that, humming away, and soon she is asleep.

Sammy is in a long tunnel. She sees a man coming toward her dressed in white. She tries to get a better look, but his face is a blur. The man vanishes.

Now she is beneath the branches of an enormous mango tree. The branches are heavy with fruit that is ripening, turning yellow. On the ground around the tree, she sees bright specks of color — little dots of green, blue, red and orange. A house with a green roof sits on hill, not far from the tree. Birds shriek.

On the top of a grassy mound, a man sits wearing a strange hat that looks like a basket and a purple loincloth. The man is brown like the earth, a short man — shorter than normal short, with spindly arms and legs, knobby knees and elbows, a potbelly and scrawny fingers. His white beard trails to the ground. The little man has a rusty short sword at his side. He takes it and points to something at the bottom of the mound. Sammy sees a door, almost hidden by the tall green grass.

She reaches for the doorknob and as she turns it, realizes there is a sign on the door that says BAWAL! — FORBIDDEN! Instead of the doorknob turning, the world spins round and round like a whirligig. It's all very scary, but she forces herself to keep her eyes open, to see it all.

Tita Patti and Tito John are on a beach talking to an old man with snow white hair and shining eyes, bluer than the blue ocean. There are palm trees, bright stars twinkling all around, and a full moon glowing behind them as they walk in the warm, foamy waves that wash the seashore. The old man points toward the dolphins and whales that break the waves, dancing and leaping in the sapphire water. His blue aloha shirt has a design of dolphins and whales.

A sleek, dark shape moves beneath the waves, pacing the old man.

The scene blurs. Sammy sees an old house. It doesn't look like a California house. The wood-framed windows are inset with little squares of mother of pearl shells. It must be a Filipino house.

Suddenly Sammy is inside, climbing a gleaming hardwood staircase. Shiny hardwood floors stretch out toward a kitchen with a long wooden table and benches.

The kitchen sink has no faucet; instead a big clay urn sits on the counter, with a tap for drawing water. An open door leads to a balcony. Next to the balcony's railing is a stone arch with a crossbeam with a bucket hanging on a long rope to bring up water from a well in the garden.

Sammy wanders through a formal dining room, large living room, sitting room and bedrooms. The man in white stands in a long hallway looking at a portrait on a wall.

The scene fades.

A little girl sits on a lawn, stringing a bracelet of beads, looking as if she thinks someone is watching her. Even though the girl never speaks, Sammy hears, *Hello Sammy*.

Like a slideshow, the scene changes again — to a man sitting in a chair with his face buried in his hands. A woman with a harsh look stands over him, pointing at him threateningly with her fan. He looks around helplessly with tears in his eyes, as if begging for someone to rescue him.

The next scene is an elderly woman with a wrinkly face, and a big lizard on her shoulder. A chain of charms dangles from her neck. A man and a woman stand beside her on a beach.

They watch a girl swim and dive in the ocean. She swims like no person Sammy has ever seen. The girl swims like a fish. It is as if she had been born in the ocean. When the girl breaks the surface, Sammy sees gills behind her ears.

Sammy begins to lose focus and the whirling stops. She awakens from her strange dream, startled and dizzy. Clambering from her bed, she falls to the floor. The thud brings her parents into her room.

Jack picks her up. "What's wrong, honey? Too excited to sleep?"

Sammy rubs her eyes. "Daddy, I had the strangest dream," she says, as he puts her back on the bed and sits beside her.

She tries to tell them everything she remembers, the man in white, the little man with the beard, the old man with Tita

Patti and Tito John on the ocean, but it all comes out in a jumble. Jack and Yvonne exchange a look.

"OK," her father says, "you're going to take a little break from fantasy books. What were you reading tonight?"

"I was reading *Snow White*. It's been a while since I've read it, and I promised my younger cousins that I would tell them the story."

As usual, Jack has a logical answer. "So, you see? The little man is one of the seven dwarves. The old woman with the lizard may have been the witch. You just dreamed your own version in your head."

"What about the other stuff?" Sammy asks. "What about the man in white?

Her mother soothes her. "Sweetheart, you're just excited about your first trip. I'll go make us some hot chocolate, OK?"

Sammy nods and snuggles up next to her father. Before Sammy can finish her chocolate drink, she nods off. Jack smoothes the bed sheet and tucks her in.

"Sweet dreams, little girl," he says. "No more weird dreams tonight. Dream about all the fun you're going to have."

Far across the blue ocean, strange forces are stirring, magical things that will soon sweep Sammy away.

In a house with wood-framed windows made of little squares of mother of pearl shells, a man wearing a white *barong Tagalog* shirt, made from pineapple fibers, sits by the window. The house is empty and the rooms are dark. He is looking at the front gate, as if expecting a visitor.

In another place, a little girl sits on a big green lawn, stringing beads for a bracelet. Other children run and shout all around her, but she pays them no mind.

A house sits on a hill, next to a huge mango tree. Next to the tree is a clump of dirt. It started out as small as a molehill, but now it grows and rumbles.

An old woman leans on a cane by the seashore, petting the lizard on her shoulder. A man and a woman, and a longhaired girl are beside her. They, too, are waiting. They look out over the vast, heaving ocean.

In Kailua on the island of Oʻahu in Hawaiʻi, an old man with a shock of white hair and deep blue eyes has fallen asleep in front of his TV set. Suddenly he feels as if a hand is shaking him urgently. He wakes up and looks about. Things whirl around him and he sees all the images that Sammy saw in her dream, one after another, exactly the same. He is deeply worried.

PATRICIA LAUREL

3

The Family

The day of departure is hectic, full of last minute errands. The condo gets a final run through with vacuuming, dusting, watering plants, brushing the kitty and finally handing over the keys to Marie Jean. Jack and Sammy go for a walk to get out of Yvonne's way.

The dream is temporarily forgotten and before she knows it, Sammy and her parents with all the boxes and their suitcases are at the airport ticket counter.

Before long other members of the family show up. They hear a shrill voice. "Hi Sammy! Look, Mom, there they are!"

Victoria waves at them.

"Victoria!" Her mother glares at her daughter. "I swear you have the mouth of a fish vendor in San Pablo."

Soon, everybody else starts to arrive. Her uncles and aunts and cousins from various parts of the Bay Area push carts full of boxes and suitcases. Victoria focuses on her other cousins and leaves Sammy.

Sammy is pleased to be alone. She takes out her new journal from her backpack. She wishes she had picked out a more subtle color than the bright pink for the journal's waterproof case. She writes down new Tagalog words and the many members of her mother's family.

Samantha Plum's Journal

Tagalog words I learned:

Kamusta? —	*How are you?*
Masarap —	*Delicious*
Pasalubong —	*Gifts you bring with you to the Philippines for family and friends*
Salamat —	*Thank you*

My mom's family: My mom has four sisters and five brothers. The sisters are Ika, Milly, Patti and Mari. My mom is the youngest. The brothers are Morris, Larry, Mike, Robert and Marc.

Most of them are married, except for Tito Morris and Tito Robert. They're both single dads. All have kids, except for Tita Patti. Tita Patti says it's enough that she has so many nieces and nephews. She can borrow them for a while as long as she can give them back to their parents. She always laughs about that.

I have many, many cousins. If I write down all their names, I won't have any room left in my journal for my adventure!

And there's Lola, of course. Lola means grandmother in Tagalog, and Lolo means grandfather. People call Lola Marita or Nene, but her real name is Maria. Lolo passed away a long time ago. His name was Bobby. Lola said he was a very nice man. I have seen pictures of him. He was very handsome. He looked mestizo. Dad says that means you're half Spanish and half Filipino. I wish I could have met my Lolo.

Mom says that we are all flying to the Philippines because of a promise they made to Lolo. Lolo also comes from a large family of 11 brothers and sisters. Each family holds a fiesta every year, and this year is our turn. They sure do have a lot of big families over there. Dad says Catholics don't believe in small families.

Thank goodness Lola only has one sister or it would be more confusing!

Mom says the reason they hold a fiesta every year during the month of May is to give thanks for a good harvest, and to show gratitude to the people who work on the farm.

My cousins tell me that I can sometimes be boring because I like to listen to adult conversations instead of playing with them. Dad says to ignore their teasing and pay attention to what the adults say.

The family started planning the fiesta a year ago. Each one was delegated an assignment. Delegate is a new word I learned. For example: Victoria likes to delegate chores because she's bossy. Here are some things that were on the list:

Children's Books	*Toys and School Supplies*
Contest Prizes	*Clothes (all sizes)*
Shoes and Slippers	*Canned Goods*
Powdered Milk	*Candies and Chocolates*
Vitamins	*Medicine*
Vegetable Seeds	*Toothbrushes*
Basketball and Net	*Old Typewriters*

Soccer Ball	*Flashlights*
Batteries	*Sheets/Towels*

These are things on the list for the people who live on the farm. The toothbrushes are for the kids so they don't lose their teeth. Mom says that most of the adults have bad teeth, but the children can be taught to care for their teeth.

The school supplies are for the daycare and elementary school. Tito Marc is bringing a couple of used typewriters for the teachers so they can prepare for classes. There are no computers on the farm.

There are other things on the list, like supplies for our families and presents or pasalubong for Lolo's brothers and sisters and other friends and relatives in San Pablo.

It looks like everybody's checked in. I'll write some more later if Victoria will let me! I bet she's sitting beside me. My other cousins will be sitting near us. Victoria always wants us to sit together so she can be in control. Might as well give in or else she'll start arguing and not leave us alone for one minute!

I can't wait to go on my first plane ride.

They're calling for the passengers to board the plane.

Goodbye, San Francisco and creampuffs. Goodbye, Kitty and Bush Street house. I'll see you in 3 weeks.

Sammy feels a hand shaking her awake. Victoria leans across her to look out the window.

"Look, is that Hawai'i? C'mon Sammy, wake up already. My mom said I should let you sleep a little more, but I think we're almost there. So, do you think that's Honolulu down there?" Victoria asks.

Sammy rubs her eyes.

She hears static and the pilot says that the plane is starting its descent. They will touch down in Honolulu in 15 minutes. The local time is 2:15 am.

"As a special treat during our layover in Honolulu, we will be able to see a total eclipse of the moon," the pilot says. "We are providing this at no extra cost to our passengers."

The cabin slowly comes alive as people prepare for arrival. Yvonne and her sister, Mari wait in line outside the toilet, talking and laughing. Everybody else is getting ready, a happy commotion all around.

Sammy has an uneasy feeling, as if something important is about to happen. Maybe it's just the excitement of flying for the first time. She looks out her window and sees the landing strip rush up.

[26]
Patricia Laurel

4

Solo

The plane lands for a 2-hour layover. The family files into the lounge area. They immediately spot Patti and John with a woman and an elderly man. They wave and a happy, noisy scene breaks out.

Sammy sees only the old man. Her family and the other people in the lounge become a blur. His presence comes into focus, like when you adjust the lens of a camera. A glow of light surrounds him, but only she can see it.

She thinks of another word she learned.

"He has an aura! Where have I seen him before?"

The man has silver hair with bright, intense blue eyes that could sparkle in the dark. He is wearing a blue cap, an ocean blue shirt designed with dolphins swimming and frolicking with whales. He holds a pair of binoculars.

"Sammy, aren't you going to say hello to Tita Patti and Tito John?" Yvonne asks.

Sammy gives her aunt and uncle a hug.

"These are our friends Nani and her father Solo," Patti says.

"Aloha and welcome to Hawai'i!" Nani says.

Sammy shakes Nani's hand and turns to Solo. When they touch, Sammy shudders and Solo's eyes light up. It is as if a jolt of electricity hit them — a shock of recognition that draws a gasp and makes your eyes go wide.

"You must be really good friends if you're willing to drive to the airport at this ungodly hour," Yvonne says.

"Believe me," Nani says. "I would have preferred to stay in bed, but my father insisted on coming here. So I volunteered to drive Patti and John."

Still holding hands, Sammy and Solo walk toward the seats by the window.

"It looks like your daughter and my father have found each other. You know, he was not feeling good earlier today. I asked him why he wanted to come and he said that he was meeting a special friend," Nani says.

The public-address system announces that the eclipse will take place in a few minutes. It is a perfect, clear night to view it from the lounge windows.

"Daddy talked about the total lunar eclipse happening when his friend arrives. He even brought his binoculars so they can watch it together. He was so adamant about coming, and there is no arguing with my father when he sets his mind on something," Nani continues.

"You know, my mother says Sammy has a sixth sense. Maybe they're here to connect," Patti says, winking at her friend.

Soon everyone scatters. Sammy's boy cousins play electronic games. The girls chase each other and giggle.

Sammy and Solo do not say anything at first. Sammy looks out the window and sees how big and round the moon is. A spreading darkness creeps to one edge.

She turns to Solo.

"Strange how things sometimes happen," he says. "Last night I had a dream about a girl. She was in some kind of trouble and I had to help her. I wasn't feeling too well this morning, but the voice in my dream said that I had to be here because something would be revealed to my friend and me. Do you think that friend is you?"

"I know where I've seen you!" Sammy says.

She tells him about her strange dream. Solo listens intently. She tells him everything. The man in white with the blurry face, the small man sitting on a mound, and the spinning whirl with all the places and faces including his.

"You're wearing a shirt with dolphins and whales all over it. That's how I recognized you," she says. "What do you think it means?"

"There's a reason why we were brought together," Solo says. "I think I'm here to be your guide for part of the journey you are about to begin."

Solo and Sammy turn to look at the moon. It is almost covered and has taken on the color of bronze. It looks like a big copper penny glowing in the sky.

"Come, Sammy." Solo says. "It's time for us to see if the moon has a message for us. We need to concentrate now."

He hands Sammy the binoculars. His eyes are very bright, almost dazzling. "Here, take this and tell me what you see. I don't need them. I can see what's up there."

The moon is covered now. Sammy looks through the binoculars.

At first, all she sees is the glowing bronze haze covering the moon. There are small black clouds floating around in slow motion. All of a sudden the clouds swirl around and form shapes. It reminds Sammy of skywriting. But instead of white writing on a blue sky, this is black on a bronze background.

The shapes are of a man bowing slightly like he is greeting someone. A very short man with a basket hat is doing a jig on top of a mound waving a little sword. A bent, old woman is walking with a cane and there is a girl beside her, a man and a woman holding hands, a little girl holding something in her hand, and other figures are coming in and out of view.

Sammy feels as if she can ask her new friend anything. "Those figures were all part of my dream! But I did not see any message. Did you? I mean, was the message supposed to be written out?"

Solo starts to turn away from the window. "I think we've seen enough. The moon is coming back."

The eclipse begins to recede. Sammy is disappointed not to know the meaning of her dream.

"Don't be sad, *keiki*. Come, we don't have much time before your plane leaves. I'll explain to you what I think the figures mean."

"I'm not a hundred percent sure," Solo says. "But I think the signs appeared tonight because they represent people you need to watch out for. Good or bad, you will find out when you encounter them. They appeared to you in a dream and then again tonight."

"What should I do when I see them? What do I do, Solo?"

"I know now that I'm to be one of your guides in this journey, but this is only our first meeting. You and I will meet again, and by then the signs will become clear to you. Now listen carefully.

"The first thing you need to do is make a list of all the things in your dream. Put a check mark beside the sign that you come across. You should put a check beside my name because we have met.

"All the signs have meaning. Write down everything you see or hear that has anything to do with your dream. Pay attention to the world, be mindful, get outside of yourself and don't be afraid to explore. Listen and learn. Use your gift."

They hear an announcement that the plane will be ready for boarding in a few minutes.

"Solo, I'm afraid I won't be strong enough. I'm only 9 years old. You said you are one of my guides. Who are the others? And what about my gift? What is it?"

"I don't know who they are. You will meet them as your journey progresses. You will also learn more about your gift."

"Solo… "

"Listen to me. You are blessed with something special that most people don't have. Don't resist it, go where your feelings take you."

Sammy looks up to see her parents, Patti and Nani approaching them.

"Did you have a good talk? Did the eclipse show you anything?" Patti asks.

"Just a few things to make life interesting," Solo says, and everybody laughs.

They walk towards the boarding gate. Sammy holds Solo's hand, afraid to let go.

"One last thing. If you are faced with a problem and you need someone to talk to, go to your Auntie Patti. She has a little of the gift you possess, and can sense some things. She turned away from it when she was a little girl, but sometimes it comes back from deep inside her," says Solo.

"Is that why you and her are so close?" Sammy asks.

Solo winks. "I saw a glimmer of it when we first met, but not as strong as yours. I also think she has a crush on me."

Patti turns to them and takes Sammy's hand. "It's time to say goodbye. Give Solo a big hug — he loves it when girls pay him attention," she says.

Sammy reaches up to embrace Solo.

"Be brave, but be careful. Remember what I said. Write everything down. Aloha, my little friend. Don't worry, our paths will cross again," he whispers in her ear.

Sammy walks away with her aunt. They turn around to wave. Sammy sees that Solo looks worn and tired.

"Don't worry, Sweetie. He'll bounce back. He needs a good rest. I think his meeting with you tired him out. You two certainly did a lot of talking. It almost made me jealous," Patti says, laughing.

"You like Solo a lot, don't you, Tita Patti?"

"We clicked instantly. There is something about Solo, I'm not sure what it is, but I think it's his aura. It surfaces from within and surrounds him. Not everyone sees it, only those that have a special bond with him," Patti says.

Soon, they are settled in their seats, and the 10-hour flight begins.

Sammy glances over at her cousin, Victoria. Good, she's finally asleep. No interruptions for a good while.

She takes out her journal and writes down everything that's happened at the airport in Honolulu. She writes down Solo's name and puts a check mark beside it. She wonders about the other images. What do they mean? Why is Tita Patti so reluctant to accept the gift? What is this gift?

Sammy leaves blank spaces between the questions for the answers that she will surely write down later.

Satisfied, she closes her journal. She turns off the light overhead, takes out her purple cuddle blanket, snuggles it to her shoulder just the way she likes it and leans back on her seat. She listens to her mother and aunts talking softly. It soothes her and before long she is asleep.

5

A Different World

The plane touches down at the Ninoy Aquino International Airport very early in the morning.

"We're 12 or 13 hours ahead of California now," Vernon says.

"I knew that," Victoria says.

After customs, they head for baggage claim. There are suitcases, but mostly huge boxes lumbering down the carousel.

"How are we going to take all those boxes to the farm? There are so many of them!" Sammy asks her mother.

"You're going to see why it took the family a year to prepare for this trip. I am sure there will be a few vans waiting for us outside," Yvonne says.

The uncles and aunts busily supervise the loading of the boxes and luggage. The older cousins keep the younger ones together, while others count all the suitcases and boxes. Next stop is the foreign exchange counter to change dollars into pesos and then to the duty free shop to buy last-minute presents.

Sammy watches the swarming carts and porters as the family prepare to head out the terminal door.

PATRICIA LAUREL

"Everyone, listen up," Larry calls out. "I have an announcement to make before we go outside."

Larry is an officer in the Air Force Reserves, and when he is put in charge of a project, suddenly it is as if he were in uniform.

His kids call it, "Daddy's military bearing."

"We are going to make a stop here in Manila before we head for San Pablo," Larry says, and everyone becomes quiet and listens. "We will stop at an orphanage where homeless and abandoned children live. Tita Ika has something very special that she wants to do there, and we have boxes of gifts for the children."

A surprise, Sammy thinks, Tita Ika has a surprise.

"I want you kids to remember," Larry says in his important, military voice, "we are not here just to have a good time. We are here because we care about people who need help, and because we want you kids to appreciate how lucky you are. This is the country of our birth, and just because we don't live here doesn't mean that we have forgotten the people."

The kids are all quiet, some of them look at the floor.

"But enough lecturing," Larry says, his voice softening. "Tita Patti's contact for the Children's Foundation should be outside waiting for us along with Lola and the rest of the family. Any questions?" He draws himself up straight again.

No questions.

"OK, let's go," Patti says. "It's going to be a long day, and we will feel the jet lag soon enough. There will be plenty of time to rest later."

Sammy is unprepared for the furnace of hot, humid air outside. Her clothes immediately cling to her skin.

I bet people take a lot of showers here, she thinks.

She looks around and there is Lola with Tita Ika, Tita Milly, Tito Morris and their families.

This is the first time Sammy sees Lola with all her children. She looks so happy. Everybody hugs.

Patti introduces Julia, the director of the Children's Foundation, and her assistant, Jocelyn.

"I am here to personally thank all of you for your generosity. I only wish more of our people living the good life elsewhere were so thoughtful," Julia says, shaking hands with everyone. "It's Sunday, so there's little traffic and driving to the Children's Home should be no problem."

"OK, let's load up!" Morris says.

Morris and Milly, along with their families say goodbye and start the long drive to the farm.

"We'll see you all in a few days," Morris says, waving as the truck full of boxes and a van with suitcases drive off.

PATRICIA LAUREL

They are soon on their way to the inner city of Manila. Sammy sees fine homes, swimming pools and manicured lawns. These neighborhoods have gates and security guards.

The van procession travels through a section of Roxas Boulevard where there is little traffic. The boulevard runs along the shoreline of Manila Bay. Sammy sees hotels, office buildings and restaurants on either side. There is a huge yacht marina with sailboats and a park. An old fortress is nearby.

"That is the walled city of Intramuros. It dates back to the Spaniards. Fort Santiago was where your great-great-great-uncle was imprisoned in the dungeon before he was executed," Lola says to her grandchildren in the van.

Everyone knows the story of Dr. Jose Rizal. Sammy has heard the story of him fighting for his people who were under the rule of tyrants.

She takes out her journal and makes a note to ask Lola more about her side of the family.

They leave the boulevard and soon the streets begin to narrow as they head toward their first stop.

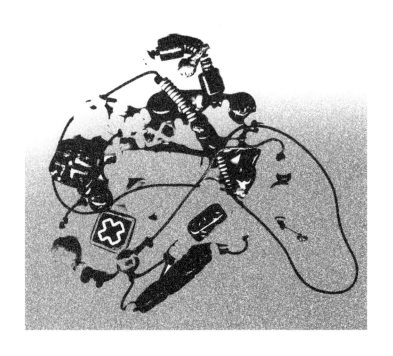

[40]
PATRICIA LAUREL

6

The Less Fortunate

Sammy watches as the Roxas Boulevard district with its tall buildings disappears. The streets are jammed with people, vehicles, heat and dirt. It is nothing like the palatial homes with lush gardens, green yards with swimming pools and shade trees they passed earlier.

The squalid buildings seem to be piled atop each other. Here people are crowded together, in cars, buses and passenger jeepneys. The noise and the exhaust from the vehicles are overpowering. Families live in tiny shacks made from packing crates and cardboard boxes. Flimsy awnings stretch over the shacks in the alleys that are alive with dogs, chickens and children barely wearing clothes.

There hardly seems any room for sunshine or a breeze. Everything is hot, noisy and stifling.

People gawk at the vans crawling through the streets. Small children begging and vendors selling pitiful wares press against the windows of the vehicles. The festering scene overwhelms them. Their guides Julia and Jocelyn warn them not to give money or buy anything as the crowd would only get worse.

They pass a muddy canal flooded by a recent rainstorm. Small children dive into the dirty water that is clotted with rotting garbage.

"Mom, why are those children swimming in that dirty water? Don't their parents know they could get sick?" Victoria asks.

"I don't know," Mari says, stunned by the scene.

Sammy watches the faces in the van. Sorrow and pity are written there. Even Victoria has nothing to say.

They pass the canal scene in silence. Someone rolls down a window.

"Whew! What is that awful smell?" Victoria asks.

Julia points at a gigantic mountain of endless, stinking garbage. "Look at this mountain of trash! The government tried to close it down because it embarrassed them. But that did not solve the problem."

Sammy holds her nose. She cannot help it. "The smoke you see is toxic fumes. There is no safe water, electricity and sewerage," says Julia. "A few years ago, the ground under the mountain of trash collapsed in a rain storm, and most of the huts and many people, including children, were buried in the tons of rubble."

The kids are very quiet now. Sammy imagines being in a storm and suddenly being washed away, buried in stinking garbage. She holds onto Victoria's hand.

"Why do the people still live there?" Victoria asks.

"Because they have no choice," Jocelyn says quietly. "They have nothing."

Sammy sees adults and children scattered on the huge wasteland, scavenging through the trash.

"What has happened to this country that was once so beautiful?" Yvonne asks.

She receives no answer.

"How do you live with this?" asks Patti.

"Ma'am, we see it every day. We have gotten used to it," says the driver.

His words sting like a slap in the face.

Yvonne watches Sammy staring at the people picking through the garbage and reaches out to comfort her. "Some of the children from the dumpsite are at the place we are going now, Sweetie. That is why we are bringing things to help them."

They drive on and come into an area with paved streets. The houses are a step up from the slapped together shacks they saw earlier.

The gloomy mood changes when Ika tells the family her big news. "I have decided to become a foster mother," she says.

She and her husband have two grown children. Ika divides her time between Germany and the Philippines. "I'm going to take in a little girl," she says, "You will all meet her at the Children's Home."

Ika's sisters are so excited, they are practically jumping up and down in their seats.

"That's right, Sweetie," Yvonne says hugging her daughter. "A new cousin for you."

Sammy can hardly find words. So much has happened since when, the day before yesterday? Her dream, the images, Solo, the long flight, the strange, bewildering sights of Manila and now this — a new cousin. What will she be like?

A few miles more and the vans stop at a tall gate. Sammy looks at the vine-covered walls. Behind them, she sees big trees, it must be a peaceful place, she thinks.

The gates open. The long driveway leads directly to the front door of an old Spanish mansion. It has a red tiled roof and two large balconies on the second floor overlooking a lush garden and playground.

Julia explains that the house was a gift from a rich man who grew up an orphan. He wanted homeless children be given a chance in life.

Children pour out of the house. They gather on the lawn and sing welcoming songs in English and Tagalog. The boys and girls are between 2 and 15 years old.

A girl and a boy holding hands step up to the front. The girl speaks in Tagalog and the boy translates. With prompting from the other kids, he delivers his carefully prepared speech with a toothy grin.

"My name is Raul and this is my friend Mayen. Thank you very much for helping us. We have no parents, but because of people like you, we will get an education and grow up to be good citizens of our country."

Raul and Mayen receive much applause.

Sammy looks at the girls, wondering who is Tita Ika's new daughter.

There are refreshments, and soon the boxes are brought out. The boxes contain backpacks in different colors filled with an assortment of school supplies and bags of sweets. There are blankets, towels, sheets, toothbrushes, soap and children's clothing.

The children sit on the lawn. They squeal with delight as they open their packs, and show each other their pencil-box sets, new notebooks and crayons.

Larry hands Julia two brown envelopes of money. One is to help the people at the dumpsite and the other is for the Children's Home.

"Dad, doesn't all this stuff cost a lot of money?" Sammy asks.

"Well, we all pooled together and started saving money for this more than a year ago. A lot of friends and family were very generous," Jack says.

Suddenly Sammy has a dreamy feeling. Everything around her seems to slow down. She can see things more precisely, as if the world is in a clearer, brighter light.

She feels as if she is watching her parents, her aunts, uncles and cousins — and the children busily unwrapping their gifts — from a distance. Almost as if she were looking down from a rooftop.

It's almost the same feeling she had when she met Solo at the Honolulu airport. Suddenly she hears a voice in her head, a girl's voice.

Sammy, the girl's voice says, *I have a gift for you. It's called an anting-anting, and it will keep you from harm.*

Sammy looks around her. She sees a girl her age sitting on the lawn, apart from the other children. She has long, straight hair and bangs cut straight across her forehead. *Here*, the voice says, *here is my gift for you, Sammy.*

The girl smiles, gazing at her with large, dark eyes.

In the corner of her eye, Sammy sees Patti staring at the girl. Tita Patti feels it too, Sammy thinks to herself.

The girl gets up and walks toward Sammy. Patti stops her. The girl opens her hand and says something. Patti beckons for Sammy to come.

Sammy walks over hesitantly, and then she hears the girl's voice in her head again. *Don't be afraid, Sammy. You'll get used to it. We can talk in a special way, that's all.*

Her aunt says, "Sammy, this is Ollie. She wants to give you something."

"I know, Tita Patti," Sammy says.

She extends her hand and Ollie gives her a bracelet made of beads.

Ollie is speaking Tagalog, and Patti translates. "The bracelet is a very special gift, Sammy, an anting-anting is a charm to..."

But all the while, Sammy hears Ollie's voice in her head.

"I know, Tita Patti. It's a magic charm, a protection from evil spirits."

"Of course," Patti mumbles to herself. "You would know that."

Ika joins them, and the adults are mystified that Sammy understands the significance of the gift.

"I just know somehow," Sammy tells them, as she and Ollie smile at each other.

You must always wear the bracelet, the voice in her head tells her.

Sammy nods at Ollie. She takes Ollie's hand and utters her first words of mind talk, *I will wear it always.*

I like this special talk, Ollie. Sammy feels giddy, like learning to walk for the first time.

Ollie smiles and nods.

Ika takes Ollie's hand and asks everyone to gather around.

"This is the girl who is going to be my new daughter. You have a new sister, a new niece, a new cousin, and a new granddaughter," Ika says smiling. Lola wipes her eyes with a white, lace handkerchief.

"Her name is Ollie," Ika says.

A great commotion now as all the Titas bend down to kiss Ollie and the Titos pat her on top of her head, pick her up, hold her high to show her off. The cousins laugh and introduce themselves one by one. Sammy hears Ollie's voice in her head, *We'll have time to talk later.*

"I visited here before, bringing things to help, and I saw Ollie. After that, I started to dream about her," Ika says. "I knew then that I was supposed to take her to live with me."

Ollie is busy kissing all her new cousins. When she put her arms around Sammy's neck, the voice in Sammy's head says, *I've dreamed about you Sammy. We have a lot to talk about. Remember, always wear the anting-anting.*

7

Lola's Hometown

Sammy's Journal...

Manila is totally different from San Francisco. It is much hotter here. The women carry fans and men have small towels wrapped around their necks. Tito Robert says it's because the towel absorbs the perspiration.

A lot of things happened today...

The family, with its newest member, leave the crowded city of Manila and head for the town of San Pablo, in the province of Laguna. They — especially the kids — are pleasantly surprised when they see the change in the landscape. The sky is so blue in the green countryside.

The group will split in two. Some will stay at Lola's house in town and the rest at a resort hotel.

The first stop is Lola's house, where the children are introduced to their grandmother's town.

Lola explains that the church was built during the Spanish rule. Of course, it has undergone many changes since. When it was renovated after World War II, nobody thought to ask who owned the land next to the church.

The house is right smack in the center of the large town next to the cathedral square. Lola said the church thought

[50]
PATRICIA LAUREL

it was their property and built a wall around it and the cathedral. By the time they discovered their mistake, it was too late.

Lola had her house built next to the church and lives under its protection, as she likes to say. At night, the cathedral gates are locked, and security guards patrol the grounds.

Everyone troops into the house to stretch their travel-weary bodies. Lola says, "Time for *merienda*." In come fruits, some they've never seen before, and other things that look like dessert placed on platters, served out on the patio. The kids think it is fun to have dessert before dinner.

Lola explains the custom of having a little something to eat between breakfast and lunch, and then again a couple of hours before dinner. "It's much like the Germans when they have cake and coffee in the late afternoon, or the English when they have afternoon tea with scones, but here we have little snacks twice a day."

The kids think it's a good thing, munching throughout the day. "As long as you don't overeat," Lola says.

The children get their first taste of exotic tropical fruits and other dishes. Some they like, and being kids, some they don't.

Sammy tries everything. First the fruit called *lanzones*. Patti had requested Lola to please find her favorite fruit. Lanzones grow on trees in bunches, much like grapes, but that's were the similarity ends. They are bigger, oblong in shape and the skin is pale yellow.

Her mother shows her how to eat the fruit. "You squeeze it in the middle, the top pops open and then you peel it. The fruit is in sections, don't swallow the seed and especially don't bite into it. The seeds are very bitter."

There are sliced mangoes, very sweet, unlike the green, yellow and red ones her mother buys at their neighborhood supermarket. She also samples the tiny sweet bananas that can be gulped down all at once.

Victoria goes for the salted peanuts mixed with fried garlic.

There are many pastries — *leche flan*, a custard dessert swimming in caramel sauce, *pastillas de leche*, sweet treats made from the milk of the carabao or water buffalo, coated with sugar and *ube*, a sweet yam pastry. After much munching, Yvonne reminds her that there is still dinner and even though she wants to keep on eating, Sammy stops herself.

Sammy feels a twinge of jet lag after the merienda, but is too excited to think about a nap. She thinks about the Energizer Bunny commercial marching around in her head and giggles to herself. It must be way past her San Francisco bedtime.

Plans are made for the next few days. Half of the group will buy supplies, as they are anxious to start preparations for the fiesta. In the morning, they leave for the farm.

The newcomers will visit the sights nearby. Sammy perks up when Lola says they will visit the *Bahay na Bato* or the House of Stone, the family's ancestral home, which is now a museum.

PATRICIA LAUREL

"Let's go to the market. We can walk off all the stuff we ate, so we can eat dinner later." Yvonne groans.

Everyone is eager to explore. They walk to the market place in the center of town. Lola stays behind with the younger cousins and the others who want to rest.

Sammy sees everyone looking at them. The large group attracts attention.

Victoria asks, "Why are people staring at us?"

"Because you dress funny," her brother Vernon says.

"Mom, tell Vernon to stop!" Victoria whines.

"Don't get her started, Vernon! I'm not in the mood for any bickering," Mari warns her children.

Shoppers jam the market. There is a huge building that the locals call the mall. It's not the kind of mall the kids are used to in California. The upper floors have small retail shops, but the lower level is jammed with side-by-side stalls. The shouts of the vendors and the jabber of the haggling shoppers create a mild uproar among the piles of fruits, meats, vegetables, house wares and clothing. It is hot and crowded and confusing.

"Everybody stay together, especially the kids. If you get lost, you won't know how to find your way back," Patti says. A couple of the adults walk behind watching for anyone who strays.

Ollie takes Sammy's hand and holds on tight. Sammy feels the little girl trembling. Ollie has never been around so many people.

Don't worry, you won't get lost. I'll make sure you're safe, Sammy says, *testing her mind talk.*

Ollie smiles.

They return to Lola's for an early dinner. As they get ready for bed, Sammy asks Ika if her new cousin could sleep with her. Ika asks Ollie and her face lights up. "*Opo*," she says. Sammy asks what it means.

"It's a respectful term for yes, especially when a younger person is addressing an older person. You'll hear it a lot," Ika says.

They all wish each other a good night's sleep.

When Sammy and Ollie get in the bed, they realize Victoria is with them.

"You didn't think I would be left out, did you Sammy?" Victoria says. "I get to sleep here too."

The bed can accommodate the three of them. They are just about to get under the thin blanket when Mari walks in. She makes the girls, amid protests especially from Victoria; take a quick shower to wash off the grimy feeling that comes from traveling. Very soon all three are fast asleep.

Sammy wakes up suddenly with a start. Her eyes slowly adjust to the darkness. A shadow looms over her. Ollie is sitting up on the bed. She is mind talking. This is so weird, she thinks.

Now listen, Ollie says. *I have something to tell you. Tomorrow we're going to visit the home of your great-great-great-great grandparents. You may see things the others can't. Don't be afraid.*

How do you know this? Sammy asks.

I dreamed it. You and I have it in us. We dream of things, and it's up to us to figure it out when we wake up. That is all I know.

How are we able to talk with our minds?

It's a gift.

From where or whom?

Ollie sighs, lies down, rolls over and sleeps.

Sammy lies in the dark thinking about what Ollie said. A lot of things are happening. Solo was right. She must be alert.

She slips out of the bed, sits on the floor and digs out her flashlight and journal from her pack, thinking about Solo's advice. She writes down everything that happened that day. Another part of her dream has become real. Ollie is the little girl in her dream. She puts a check beside Ollie's name in her book.

So many questions still need answers. What is this gift and what am I suppose to do with it? Why am I able to mind talk with Ollie? Why me? she asks herself before sleep takes over.

A rooster crows somewhere and they are awake. Lola's dogs bark in the yard, excited because there are so many new people in the house.

They hear a clatter in the kitchen. The three girls come out in their pajamas, rubbing their eyes.

"Here are the three little sleepyheads," Lola says, smiling at them. "Everyone else is ready to eat, are you?"

"You bet we are, Lola," Sammy says, looking at the table covered with fresh fruit and all sorts of breakfast fare.

"Good, Lola says. "After breakfast, we will visit the house of your ancestors.

Bahay Na Bato
House of Stone

The family drives to the town of Calamba to visit their ancestral home, which is now a museum. Lola says the architects did a very good job with the reconstruction based on old photographs and paintings.

The museum's curator meets the family at the front gate. In Tagalog the term *Bahay na Bato* is used for older homes built during the Spanish years. The curator relates the history of the house and the people who lived in it. Lola's stories of the family begin to come alive for the kids.

As the family enters, the curator steps away from them to give a lecture to a group of school children.

"Let's stand here and listen a moment," says Lola. "It's important for the young ones to hear this."

Sammy listens to her grandmother, journal and pen at the ready.

"Dr. Jose Rizal is considered the national patriot of the Philippines," the curator says. "He was a doctor, a novelist and a poet. He is regarded as one of the noblest figures Asia has produced. His writings inspired the revolution against the Spanish colonialists."

"Is there a statue of Dr. Rizal in your town?" she asks the children.

PATRICIA LAUREL

All of the children nod.

"There are statues of Dr. Rizal in towns and cities all over the Philippines," the curator says.

"He is our national martyr, executed by the Spanish rulers on December 30, 1896 after a long exile and imprisonment. His poem written before his execution "Mi Ultimo Adios" or "My Last Farewell" is his final known literary work."

"Wow!" Victoria whispers to Sammy. "Is that OUR ancestor she's talking about?"

"Yes, Victoria," Lola says in a low voice. "Dr. Rizal was my great-uncle and your and Sammy's great-great-great uncle."

The curator overhears and turns to Lola. "It would be an honor if you would relate to us the story of how Dr. Rizal's siblings smuggled his final poem out of prison, Ma'am."

The fascinated school children nod, their eyes big and round. The curator, smiling her assent, graciously makes room for Lola, who begins to relate the story...

"My great-grandmother, Teodora Alonso was Dr. Rizal's mother. On the eve of his execution, Teodora Alonso went to visit him for the last time. My Uncle Morris was just a boy. He and his mother, Maria went along. They were not allowed to enter his cell at the same time.

"Dr. Rizal's mother was the first to go in. Next to follow were Morris and his mother. He was given a pocket watch by his beloved uncle. The other aunts followed and received other articles belonging to Dr. Rizal. One

Chapter 8 ~ Bahay Na Bato, House of Stone

was a lantern. As he did not want the Spanish guards to hear what he had to say, our Lolo Pepe whispered to his sisters in English that they were not to light the lantern, but instead, to look inside it when they got home. There were tearful goodbyes, then the final leave taking. They returned home with heavy hearts."

Here the storyteller stops and looks around at her captive audience. "What happened next?" an excited student blurts out.

Lola lets the suspense build, then continues. "Sure enough, when the lantern was opened, out fell a piece of paper, which had been folded several times. The family carefully unfolded the document and discovered the final poem of the man who was about to give his life in the name of freedom."

The school children break into a spontaneous round of applause. As the students resume their tour, the curator returns to Lola and her group.

As they walk through the house, the curator says, "There are people who swear the spirits of your ancestors still occupy these rooms."

Sammy asks, "Do you believe this?"

"Yes, of course," is the curator's emphatic reply.

Her favorite story: One day a week the house is closed to the public. She was upstairs in the living room. She felt a breeze even though the air was very still in the house.

"Suddenly I felt a light touch. It felt like someone with very cold hands touched me on the back of my neck. There was no one else with me. I froze, but I wasn't frightened. I felt like someone was thanking us for taking care of the house."

Sammy feels the hairs rise on her arms and the back of her neck as they pass through the double wooden doors. She recalls Tita Patti's term for goose bumps in Hawai'i. The locals call it chicken skin.

She holds on to Ollie's hand.

Don't worry, we are in the land of your family stories, and this is a good place with a story all its own. It won't scare you, but I think it might make you a little sad, Ollie whispers in Sammy's mind.

They pass through the lower level. The curator tells them it was probably used to house the servants and a horse and carriage. There are paintings and photographs on the walls. The floor on this level is the only remaining part of the original house.

There is an artist's sketch of a horse drawn carriage with a man sitting inside wearing a derby hat and a suit. Two men and several women stand beside the carriage.

The women are in long skirts with full butterfly sleeves and neck scarfs over their shoulders. Some of them hold Spanish *abanicos* or fans. These days Filipinos call them *pamaypay*. The dress is called the *Maria Clara*.

The two men wear loose-fitting *barong Tagalog* over trousers.

The sketch depicts Dr. Rizal's return from Madrid, where he was studying. Welcoming him are his parents, older brother and sisters.

Suddenly, the gallery of photographs and paintings, along with Sammy's family and the curator, disappear. She looks around, wondering where everyone went.

She stands next to a carriage. The place is busy with two women doing household chores. They wear long skirts like in the painting, but not as fancy.

One woman sweeps while the other polishes the red stone floor with the half shell of a coconut. She has one foot on the floor and the other on the shell. One hand holds her long skirt up slightly and the other hand is behind her back. She pushes across the floor in a gliding motion on one foot, and switches to the other, as if she were skating.

The coconut half shell is called a *bunot* and the oil from the shell makes the floor gleam.

The women pay no attention to Sammy. It is as if she weren't there. It all seems so strange. A little panic, but she stifles it and decides to take a look around.

She proceeds cautiously up the gleaming hardwood staircase. She looks back at the woman with the coconut shell and wonders how long it will take to clean the stairs and the rest of the house.

I hope they take turns, she thinks.

Sammy pauses at the top of the stairs.

Straight ahead is a kitchen and an informal dining room with a long wooden table and benches. Two women busily prepare a meal. They wear the same type of clothing, only finer than the two downstairs. One is Lola's age and the younger one looks like her daughter.

A big ceramic jug with a spigot for water is perched on a stand in a corner. It must be hard work to lug buckets of water up the stairs. Sammy has never seen such kitchen utensils. The stone counter facing the window is the cooking area. Clay pots sit atop a stack of bricks with red coals underneath. Just like the others downstairs, the two women do not notice Sammy.

I wonder who they are?

Sammy goes to the balcony. A bucket hangs on a rope from a stone arch. She looks down over the railing to see a well in the garden. The bucket is lowered, filled with water and pulled up by rope.

This is the house in my dream!

There are two closets side by side. She looks inside. One is a toilet with a bucket of water beside it. Flushing must not be invented yet, she thinks. The other closet has a marble stand with a basin and pitcher of water and a mirror hanging on the wall. This must be where they wash their faces and brush their teeth.

Chapter 8 ~ Bahay Na Bato, House of Stone

She wonders how they take showers. Maybe they have a bathtub somewhere. Or maybe they just take sponge baths. Lola said that's how they used to wash themselves during World War II when there was no running water.

Sammy goes back inside. The entire upper floor has sliding, *capiz* windows. Each wooden framed window has an inset of small, polished squares of mother-of-pearl shells to let in the light.

She turns around and sees a woman with two children, a girl and boy in the formal dining room. The woman arranges flowers on the large dining table. Fine china and silverware are in place.

It looks like they are preparing for a huge dinner.

Sammy approaches the children. They look longingly at the *bahay kubo* in the garden and then back at the woman, hoping she gets the hint. Sammy knows how they feel. I would want to play outside instead of being in the house. She thinks they are well behaved compared to her rowdy cousins.

The children don't notice her. I must be invisible to them.

She feels like a ghost from the future.

Someone's eyes are on her. She turns around. They stare at each other in amazement.

Paciano Rizal is taller than most Filipino men. He has fair complexion and a long face with high cheekbones. Lola has the same face, our Chinese heritage, she calls it.

He wears a white *barong Tagalog* and holds a newspaper. The other hand covers his mouth as if he is keeping himself from shouting.

Panic is not something the family needs now. With the serious problems they face, they all must be calm.

Oh yes, the calm before the storm, he thinks. His brother's outspokenness brought the Spanish friars' wrath on him and the family. If anything, the blame should be mine.

He was the driving force behind his younger brother, Pepe. He was responsible for sending his brother to study abroad and strongly advised him to publicize the atrocities the friars were inflicting on the people. Pepe did just that. He wrote not only the first book, but also a second one that angered the friars.

Maybe Pepe should have stayed away, Paciano thinks. But then he knows that was out of the question. His brother felt it was his duty to face the friars and their accusations of treason.

That's absurd. Foreigners accusing a native son of treason, he thinks.

Sammy sees the date on the newspaper — June 1892!

The man looks at his niece and nephew by the window, and then at this strange girl, scrutinizing her clothes, her bare legs and sandals. She wears shorts and T-shirt with her backpack slung on one shoulder. Where is this child from?

This must be Lolo Ciano, Sammy thinks. There were two sons and nine daughters in this family. Sammy had seen many photos of the famous son, Pepe the doctor. But only one photo of Lolo Ciano, the only photo in existence, and she knows this is that man.

She remembers Lola telling her the story behind the photo. Lolo Ciano was standing in front of what looked like a decorative tablecloth. He was not looking at the camera, but at the object in front of him.

Once during a family gathering, Lola showed the photo to a friend, and asked her friend to guess what the object was in front of Lolo Ciano. A tablecloth, was the reply.

Lola laughed and revealed that it was her mother's backside. Her mother was bending down right when the photo was snapped. "Isn't that funny? The only known photo of my great-uncle, and my mother's butt is in it."

How can Lolo Ciano see me when the others can't? Sammy wonders. Does he have the gift too?

He looks from her to the two children again. He rubs his eyes. The vision doesn't go away.

Sammy opens her mouth to say something, but he puts a finger to his lips and motions her to follow him to the living room, away from his sister and her two children.

Lolo Ciano bows toward her as though they are being introduced. Just like the image of the man she saw on the copper moon in Hawai'i.

She tries mind talk. *Are you Lolo Ciano?*

More amazement on his face. A member of the family, maybe from another time? She has the gift.

Is this how they dress little girls where you come from, child?

Yes, Lolo Ciano.

And where may that place be?

San Franciscio, California, Lolo Ciano.

Lolo Ciano appears startled, but composes himself. *Are you from my line, child?*

Sammy says her mother is Yvonne, whose mother is Marita, the daughter of Encarnacion, the daughter of Maria, his sister.

What is your name, child?

She tells him her name is Samantha, but people call her Sammy or Sam. He says that sounds like a boy's name.

That doesn't matter so much in my time, Lolo Ciano, she says.

Her time, the man turns that over in his mind. *I prefer to call you Samantha.*

This child, even though she is very young, may know the future of his family, how their lives may play out.

Listen, to me, Samantha. This is most important.

Sammy nods solemnly.

Chapter 8 ~ Bahay Na Bato, House of Stone

I do not understand everything that is going on here. I assume you do not, either.

Sammy nods again.

I know something very important is destined for my brother Pepe. I am sure it involves great sadness. I have seen some of it in dreams. Have you ever had such dreams?

Yes, Lolo Ciano.

I suspected as much. Listen to me carefully. You must not tell me anything about the future. We cannot avoid our destiny. Not just our family, but also millions of our countrymen will be affected by all this. It has to play itself out as it has been ordained by history. Do you understand?

Sammy nods again.

Promise me.

I promise, Lolo Ciano.

I think I will find out soon enough even if it's something that I dread. I know that my younger brother's life is in danger, but it would not be right to tamper with whatever the future holds for him or any of us in the family.

We're getting ready for Pepe's welcome home dinner. The woman in the dining room is your great-great grandmother Maria. See the girl and boy by the window? The girl is your great grandmother, Encarnacion and the boy is her brother Morris.

Sammy walks over to her family, choking back emotions. Trying to stay calm.

She approaches Lola Maria. She sees all the women in the family in her face. She looks sad. Sammy remembers her mother's story of Lola Maria. She was the first independent woman in the family. She left her husband, Lolo Daniel. He disappointed her too many times. She tolerated his gambling and philandering for as long as she could. He did not take her threats seriously until she and the children finally left for good.

Her spinster sisters did not treated Lola Maria, and especially her children, very kindly. No matter how bad the marriage, people stayed together in those days.

Sammy turns her attention to the children looking out the window. Lola Encarnacion looks to be some years younger than Sammy. Lolo Morris is the younger of the two. They seem very protective of each other. Sammy knows they will remain so until the end of Lolo Morris' life during World War II. She feels a sudden sadness for the boy by the window.

The two women in the kitchen enter the dining room. They announce that the meal will be served shortly. The older woman says something to Lolo Ciano and disappears into one of the rooms in the house.

Lolo Ciano tells Sammy that the older woman is his mother, Teodora. *My father Francisco is the head of this house, but my mother holds the family together.*

He tells Sammy that he will introduce the relatives as they come in.

Voices float into the dining room. Sammy's family is sitting down to dinner.

What she is seeing is too incredible. Who would believe her? Solo and Ollie would and maybe Tita Patti — maybe. Anyone else would think she was hallucinating.

Her great-great-great-great grandparents are first, followed by their children. Lola Teodora, the matriach of the family, leans on her husband Lolo Francisco's arm. She squints her eyes, trying to focus on her surroundings. Sammy knows that she had been going blind before her son Pepe operated on her. Lolo Ciano tells Sammy who each person is.

Sammy pays particular attention to her great-great-grandmother, Maria and her daughter, Encarnacion. She studies their faces and their movements. *My girl cousins and I look like them. I can see all of us in the way they look, walk and talk.* Sammy watches Lola Encarnacion bending over her little brother Morris, talking in whispers so as not to be heard by the adults.

Sammy cannot take her eyes off the family's pride, Lolo Pepe. She is looking at the man whose courage and sacrifice helped end more than 400 years of Spanish rule. She is seeing the hero for herself. She has seen his face in her uncles.

They all pass her. She wants so much to reach out to them, to touch them, but something tells her not to.

PATRICIA LAUREL

When everyone is settled, Sammy stands beside Lolo Ciano's chair. She notices the children — funny how she thought of her great-grandmother and her brother as kids — are led to a separate table near the kitchen by a woman who is probably their *yaya*.

Sammy remembers her mother's stories about the yayas who took care of her and her brothers and sisters. "They hung around us all the time," her mother said. "In a way, they were also the ones that helped shape our characters. You needed a good *yaya* to show you the way."

Sammy realizes that she may be witnessing the family's last time together. The newspaper Lolo Ciano had was dated June 1892. This must be before Lolo Pepe was exiled by the Spanish to the distant island of Dapitan. She is glad she has read about the family's history.

If only she could tell Lolo Ciano, but his warning sounds an alarm in her brain. If she says anything now, history will change. She keeps her knowledge of the future to herself.

The atmosphere seems tense. They all look up with apprehension every time they hear the door open downstairs.

Finally, Lola Teodora says, "Let us make the most of our time together. We will deal with it when and if they come for Pepe. I will not have this food wasted."

Sammy is pleasantly surprised that she can smell the aroma of the steaming dishes brought out and set on the table. She is getting hungry.

The conversation becomes animated. Pepe entertains them with stories of Europe and the people he met. He turns to his sister Maria and says, "You are so stubborn and headstrong that you would feel right at home in Germany, sister — if you had been a man!"

Everyone laughs.

Lola Maria takes her brother's remark as a compliment. "I'm sure I could teach those Germans a thing or two!"

Pepe turns his attention to his older brother. He has a curious look on his face.

Sammy feels like Lolo Pepe is staring right at her. She looks around her to see if anyone else is beside her. Lolo Pepe says, "I sense a presence beside you, Kuya Ciano, but I think it is a good one. Maybe we have a guardian angel in our midst. Maybe this angel will protect our family?"

But Lolo Ciano looks as if he is about to fall off his chair. He turns to his brother and asks, "Can you see her?" At the same time Sammy is asking, *Lolo Ciano, does Lolo Pepe have the gift too?*

There is a loud commotion outside the house. The family falls silent. They hear horses, shouted orders, a booming knock on the door, footsteps tramping up the stairs.

A servant announces the name of a Spanish officer. He looks around the table. He walks over to Lolo Pepe and says, "Señor, you are ordered to report immediately to…"

Sammy runs to Lolo Pepe and reaches out.

He disappears; instead Patti has her arms around her.

Sammy is torn away from the scene, wondering what happened in that dining room so many years ago.

She realizes that next time she visits the past, she shouldn't touch anyone — I probably shouldn't have touched Lolo Pepe.

Sammy feels stinging tears. She wipes her face, but not before Patti sees.

"Sammy, are you OK? You were standing by the table like you were in a trance. Is there something you want to tell me?"

Sammy's voice is shaky. "I'm not sure. Did anyone notice anything?"

"No. The others are too busy looking around."

"How long was I gone?"

"It was only for a few minutes. What's wrong?"

"Did you touch me?"

"Well, yes. When I saw you scared and crying."

"Did you see something, Tita Patti?"

That's what brought her back. Her aunt touched her. She isn't sure if she should be angry or relieved. Maybe she wasn't meant to see what happened next.

"No, well… a glimpse maybe. I saw people… "

"I knew it! I have to tell Ollie. You know about Ollie, don't you?"

"OK, sweetie. Try to calm down."

She hugs her aunt. Solo was right. Her aunt has the gift, but she is not ready to deal with it.

Patti changes the subject. "Don't you think it's time for lunch? I need to remind the others that we are expected for lunch at Lolo Ciano's old rest house in Los Baños. His grandchildren invited us to eat with them."

"We're going to meet Lolo Ciano's family? Wow, that would be great."

"C'mon, let's go look for the others," Patti says.

They drive to the town of Los Baños. The grandchildren of Lolo Ciano warmly greet them. One of them, Lolo Fran, particularly resembles his grandfather. They tour the house by the Laguna de Bay.

Sammy sees the only photo of Lolo Ciano. She is amused that he is looking at her great grandmother's backside. Lola tells the story of the photo again.

Back at the *Bahay na Bato*, Lolo Ciano materializes. He blinks and looks around. But where is he? He knows he's in the future, and the house has a different feel and look.

Ah yes, the old house was burned to the ground.

He hears the sound of many footsteps on the stairs. Are the Spaniards still here? He looks about frantically when a group of students and their teacher walk past, around and through him.

Lolo Ciano listens to the teacher talk about his family.

Where is that little girl, that girl Samantha?

On the way back to San Pablo, Sammy takes out her journal. She puts a check mark beside Lolo Ciano's name. She feels they will meet again very soon. Now she knows three of her guides.

[76]
PATRICIA LAUREL

Something Evil in the Works

Evil lurks, waiting to spring on its prey. Evil bides its time, waiting for the right moment to take its victim unawares, just as the cobra watches and flicks its forked tongue.

As Lola's family plans its joyous reunion and fiesta, someone, driven by jealousy and resentment, plots against them.

Her name is Jenny, and she is one of Lola's nieces. She comes from a part of the family that thinks it can never have enough of anything, especially money.

Jenny nurtures the blind animosity and jealousy, cherishes it.

For years her malicious gossip, her mean little tricks, her slights and snubs have had little effect. Now she is ready to strike. Jenny has a strong feeling that at last her time has come to spread venom among her aunt and cousins. She is the secret cobra in the family.

One day before the fiesta, Jenny visits the farm. The workers avoid her and show themselves only if she calls. Her uncles, aunts and cousins steer clear as well.

She feels best when she orders people around. Jenny likes to use Spanish words that are lost on the people who live on the farm. It gives her a sense of superiority.

It irritates her that she has to climb the hill to Milly's house. What is this hill doing here in her way? Why did stupid Milly have to build her house on a hill? In her thinking, all of this land should by rights belong to her.

By the time she reaches the house, Jenny is huffing, puffing and bathed in sweat. She sits on the porch and fans herself furiously. Her *abanico*, she calls the fan, using the Spanish word.

It doesn't help her mood any, looking around the place. Her cousin's vacation home is happily situated on one of the choicest spots on the farm. The house overlooks miles of coconut trees and the China Sea. It looks very peaceful. It is also breezier than her house further down the hill. No air circulates around her house, especially during the summer. Flies and the occasional gecko are the only things that breeze in and out of her stifling house. Sometimes a cobra slinks in, causing much excitement.

Her burning resentment focuses on her cousin Milly. She also has her eye on the houses a little further down. Ika's house and the house recently built by Patti and Yvonne.

Hmm... a little grass fire would take care of these three houses, she thinks.

Her cousins have people living on the premises and they are always on their guard. This does not sit well with Jenny. Her beady eyes turn to the couple busily cleaning Milly's house.

PATRICIA LAUREL

"*Hoy!*" Jenny's shrill voice shatters the quiet of the afternoon.

The two unsuspecting workers look up. Fear shows on their faces. This pleases Jenny tremendously. Side by side, almost cowering, the couple approach her.

"Good afternoon, Ate Jenny," the man says respectfully, trying not to look at her. Jenny resents being called *Ate*, she prefers to be called *Señora*, but it's no use. No matter how many times she tells these farm people, they forget.

"Why did you not respond immediately when I called you? What goes on here?" Jenny asks, pointing her *abanico* threateningly.

"Sorry, Ate Jenny. We did not hear you. We are getting the house ready. Ate Milly and her family are arriving today. They're arriving early so they can prepare for the fiesta. The others will be coming in a few days."

Jenny thinks about ordering the couple to do something for her, but knows she will get in trouble with Milly. Instead she sits on a wooden bench on the porch and orders the wife to get her something to drink and a snack. She might as well get something in return for the grueling climb up the hill. She dismisses the husband with an irritated wave of her hand.

Might as well sit and enjoy the view. I never feel welcome when they're here, she thinks grudgingly.

She senses rather than sees the movement behind the huge mango tree, a stone's throw from the house.

There! What was that? Some misshapen thing looking at her?

"*Hoy*! Come over here at once!" Jenny shrieks.

The air seems to glimmer and shimmer. The light hurts her eyes and the sun feels even hotter, more intense, beating down on her. Jenny stirs the air with her *abanico*, but it does no good. She feels like someone in the desert who is about to witness a mirage.

Still fanning herself furiously, Jenny walks toward the mango tree.

The shimmering heat opens like a curtain. A very short man steps out. He has a long beard, a pot belly and skinny legs with knobby knees. He is brown like the earth and wears a basket hat made from dried mango peels, a purple loincloth and carries a sword.

He approaches Jenny. Her senses tell her to be afraid of this strange little man. But she stays put. She stands with arms crossed and pretends to fear nothing.

"Who are you? I've never seen you before. Whom do you work for?" Jenny demands.

"I should have met you when you were younger, you would have made an eager apprentice," the little man says, chuckling.

Jenny sets her jaw. "Nobody makes an apprentice out of me!"

They circle one another, eyes locked.

The little man introduces himself. "You've heard stories about me when you were a child and I'm sure you haven't forgotten who I am. I'm buried deep in the memory of all who know me. I am what you humans call a *duwende*, and not just any *duwende*. I come from Spain."

"Should I be impressed?" But Jenny knows the *duwende* is an enchanted creature of the earth. And Jenny loves Spain; perhaps this a lucky omen. She stands defiantly, hands on hips, biding her time.

"You do have the air of a Señora," the *duwende* says, bowing.

Jenny puffs up. She is pleased that this small man knows his place.

The *duwende* admires Jenny's coarseness. He can make this human his ally. He has been watching her for a long time and he senses her weakness. He knows how she can be used.

Greed blinds her, the *duwende* tells himself.

They talk some more, probing, testing each other warily. The *duwende* has the advantage because he knows more about Jenny than she knows about him. This irks her. She tries to recall all the stories she heard about these enchanted creatures and their strange powers. How can she use him to hurt her cousins and gain more for herself?

The *duwende* wants to enlist Jenny's aid in punishing someone who got away from him many years ago. He tells

Chapter 9 ~ Something Evil in the Works

her the story of a beautiful little girl he wanted to steal and keep all for himself, like a lovely bird in a cage. But she escaped him. Now she is an adult and has a daughter.

"A daughter just as beautiful," he says. "They will be coming for the fiesta along with the rest of their family. This will be her first time back since her escape."

Jenny asks him who this person is. He tells her. Her eyes widen and she claps her hands with joy. Oh, she is so happy. "Of course, I will help you," she says excitedly. The *duwende* laughs at her change of tune.

He tells Jenny all he needs is time alone with the little girl to cast his spell.

Jenny asks him what he is willing to pay. The *duwende* asks her price.

"I want my aunt and cousins and other relatives evicted from the farm," she says.

A giant electric company wants to build a power plant in the area and would pay a huge price for the land. She believes the farm would be an ideal location, but she leaves out this bit of information.

"I want to be the sole owner of all this," Jenny says.

The *duwende* gives her a leering grin, and they laugh.

She says she will bring the little girl to him. What she wants in return is the free and clear title of the farm. Because he has magical powers, it should be no problem.

"But should you fail," the *duwende* points his sword up at her menacingly, "should you fail, I will make you answer for it."

Jenny feels her heart pounding. "Don't worry," she says, her voice trembling slightly. "I always get what I want, and stop pointing that old sword at me."

"It's a cutlass," the *duwende* says, "I carried it aboard the galleon when I came over with the Spanish."

He lowers the cutlass. "Do not fail, my Jenny," the *duwende* says, smiling.

He reaches up, touching her forehead.

Jenny feels a burning sensation. "What did you just do?"

"Oh, I just put a little mark on you. It is a reminder of the work ahead, so you don't forget our agreement. It will disappear once you accomplish your task," he says.

The mark is a tiny black mole. Jenny can feel it. She touches her finger to it and sees the duwende disappearing behind the mound beside the mango tree.

"So, that's where you live," Jenny thinks to herself. She will have to do some serious research on *duwendes* and their magic. She takes out a compact mirror from her skirt pocket and looks at the small, black mark. Not too bad, people will think it's a beauty mark. She snaps the compact shut and walks down the hill, humming to herself.

Another happy thought occurs to her. Milly's place is not so peaceful after all. Unpleasantness lurks by her mango tree. All she has to do is wait.

What Jenny does not know is that now the *duwende* can reach her anywhere. If she fails, he will be able to punish her.

On the Way to the Farm

The day arrives to drive to the farm. Three vans carry everyone and the supplies.

They must start early to reach the farm during daylight, so they leave San Pablo in darkness. Vernon and Victoria snuggle in their seats and go back to sleep. The adults are groggy, so there is little talk. Only Sammy and Ollie in the back are wide-awake. Sammy practices her mind talk.

Ollie, where did you come from? Do you have parents?

All I know is that I was left outside the gate of the orphanage. No one knows who my parents are. But there are voices in my head that tell me that one day, I will see them again.

Will they take you away from Tita Ika?

I don't know. Right now, I feel I was meant to be with you and your family. Mama Ika taking me in is all part of a plan. I'm not yet sure what the plan is.

Ollie explains to Sammy that the voices in her dreams have been telling her what to do ever since she can remember.

Do you know whom these voices belong to?

No, but there are two voices, a man and a woman. They come from far away. In my dreams, I see a small house with a stream flowing by it and plants everywhere. It looks like a happy place.

[86]
PATRICIA LAUREL

Maybe you'll find out one day, Ollie. Now I know that you and I share this gift of mind talking, and we have dreams that become real. I still have a ways to go to figure out my weird dream.

Sammy tells Ollie everything that's happened — her dreams, meeting Solo and Lolo Ciano.

I cannot see your Lolo Ciano, but I felt his presence when we visited the House of Stone. I have a feeling that something is going to happen. I'm not sure it's good.

Don't worry, Ollie. We've got each other. Together we can solve whatever problems come our way. Besides we've got a huge family that will protect us.

Sammy pats her friend on the shoulder.

If someone were awake, they would think it odd that the two girls sitting in the back are wide awake and not talking, but their faces are full of expressions and sometimes they gesture with their hands.

Sammy tells stories about their large family.

It's good for you to know since you are now part of it. OK, now it's your turn. Tell me a story about the time you spent at the orphanage.

Ollie tells Sammy about a trip she made with the other kids from the orphanage. They had an outing, a road trip, to see the sights in Manila. Ollie sat on a bench in a large park. The park was jammed with workers busily strolling through, street children running and playing, vendors and beggars.

The soot and smoke of diesel exhaust from cars, buses and jeepneys hung in the air. It was hot and noisy, and the relentless traffic raised a wave of ceaseless, grating clamor.

She sat in the shade cast by a statue of the national hero, a dignified man in a suit, who held a book in one hand. Ollie watched the other orphans play, so happy to be out in the park, ignoring all the noise and heat.

She felt a presence before her and looked up to see a fierce looking man in tribal clothing. Looking closer she realized he was more sad than fierce, that he had the perplexed look of someone whose pride had been wounded.

Ollie realized that he was Datu Lapu Lapu, who defeated Ferdinand Magellan, the Spanish explorer, when he tried to conquer the Datu's island of Mactan more than 400 years ago.

Another man appeared.

He was dressed in old-fashioned European clothing. It was the man whose statue presided over the park, Dr. Jose Rizal. *(Sammy, it was your uncle!)* He studied abroad and wrote about the atrocities his people suffered under Spanish rule.

An old woman appeared with other Filipino heroes. She was known as Tandang Sora or Old Sora, the Mother of the Philippine Revolution. Secret meetings of the rebel organization, Katipunan were held in her home. The old woman had tears in her eyes.

PATRICIA LAUREL

"What happened here?" Tandang Sora asked.

Ollie looked about her, but saw nothing out of the ordinary. Just a beaten-dirt park with trees, benches, a playground. And beyond it the teeming streets, the traffic, the noise, the smeared greasy blackness hanging low in the sky, the tottering cardboard shacks where people live jammed against each other, the streets and sidewalks piled high with trash and garbage, and so many people, ragged and poor, milling about.

Dirty children flagging pitiful goods at the passing cars, trying to earn a few pesos, women clutching babies, shooing flies away. The haze of the heat and smog everywhere.

"Child, can't you see it?" Datu Lapu Lapu asked. He seemed even more upset that Ollie considered what she saw as normal, as the way things should be.

Ollie noticed for the first time a mountain of trash peaking up beyond a stonewall along one side of the park.

"This is much worse than dying for your country," Tandang Sora said, wringing her hands. "Are our people so blind?"

They all stood silent. Then Dr. Rizal said, "What about you, child, will you do something? It's your country now."

"But it's not up to me. I'm just a child. Nobody will listen to me," Ollie said.

"You may be surprised at what a young child can do. If you and your friends voice your fears, the adults may just be shamed into doing something," Dr. Rizal said.

Ollie thought about that. Why shouldn't children band together and make adults aware that they are responsible for the poverty and destruction to the environment? They should clean up the earth for the future generations.

Before she could respond to Sammy's uncle, the ghost heroes and heroine melted away in the haze.

Dr. Rizal was the last to go. He turned around and smiled. "Don't worry, there are people who will listen and help," he said.

Ollie was suddenly alone.

Wow, that must have been something! Sammy says, after hearing her friend's story. *We should talk to my aunts and uncles. I bet they can help us come up with ideas.*

We can start small. With the help of the adults, we can teach people how to care for the land and the sea, Ollie says.

OK, we'll talk to them.

Everyone in the van stirs. The two girls end their mind talk. Patti, who is in the seat in front of them, raises her head and looks at her niece. She winks at her.

Tita Patti wasn't sleeping! She heard us, Ollie.

I know. She knows more than she lets on.

Patti turns around and whispers to Sammy. "I caught a little bit of your conversation. This mind talking thing, I catch bits and pieces. It's a lot like listening to a radio with static."

Before Sammy can respond, Patti puts a finger to her lips to silence her. "We'll discuss this later when we're alone, OK?"

Sammy nods her head. She grins at Ollie. Her circle is getting bigger.

"OK, kids we're approaching the winding hill called *Bituka nang Manok*. It's a national park," Yvonne says.

"The what?" Victoria asks.

"The translation is really yucky, but the driver says that is how the locals describe the hill we are climbing. It literally means the insides of a chicken. Maybe it's because the road is winding up and down, I don't know. I've never seen the insides of a chicken," Yvonne says with a laugh.

"Do you see those people lined up all along the steepest part of the hill? They make their living waving the motorists through the most treacherous parts. When they wave, that means it is safe to continue because there is no oncoming traffic. The motorists thank them by throwing money," Mari says.

"Oooh, my ears are popping," Vernon says as the van climbs the hill. The driver turns off the air-conditioning in case the engine overheats.

They roll down the windows. The kids are given coins to throw to the people. They are warned not to throw paper money as the wind will blow it away. It is dangerous if one of them should run and slip and fall into one of the ravines.

"It feels like we're slowly going up and down on a roller coaster," Vernon says, as he throws coins.

Sammy looks out over the deep ravine that seems to go on forever. Soon they start their descent and are once more back on the highway. The driver looks more relaxed.

They stop for lunch at a restaurant in the seaside town of Gumaca. A delicious aroma greets the hungry travelers. The menu offers tantalizing choices of meats, chicken, fish, noodles, steamed and fried rice and vegetables.

After lunch, the kids are introduced to a dessert called *halo-halo*. Patti says it is like the Hawaiian shave ice, but different. Shave ice comes in different colors and flavors and sometimes, depending on your taste, they serve it with ice cream and sweet beans. The halo-halo has all sorts of stuff in it.

The waiter comes out with tall, clear glasses that show off the colorful contents of the halo-halo. Sammy writes down the ingredients in her journal while eating the strange dessert.

Lola explained to us that halo-halo means a mixture of anything, like food, for example. She says it is a favorite Filipino dessert especially during the hot months. It is very filling. Since they come in huge portions, we are going to share the halo-halo.

OK, here goes.

These are the ingredients:

Sweet preserved beans like red beans and chickpea (sounds yucky), macapuno — coconut meat, langka — jackfruit, pinipig — pounded dried rice, (Mom says they're like rice crispies only a little harder), leche flan — custard flan, saba — a type of banana, jello pieces, crushed ice, milk or coconut milk. All in a tall glass topped with vanilla or ube — sweet yam ice cream.

It's good they don't tell you the ingredients. After you have a taste and like it, then you can ask what it's made of. Then you won't mind too much if you just ate beans for dessert!

After lunch, back in the van, Mari says they should reach the town of Tagkawayan in a little more than an hour.

Sammy listens to her mom and aunts talking and laughing. She remembers one time when all the sisters and Lola were together in San Francisco. That was when Lola lived in an apartment near them.

They spent hours sitting in Lola's living room gabbing. She and Victoria loved to listen to the stories, tales that became juicier with every retelling.

John says it's called talk story in Hawai'i.

The talk soothes the three girls. They sit mesmerized, infected by the sisters' laughter.

PATRICIA LAUREL

The Farm

The vans turn onto a narrow road with rice fields on either side.

The roads are paved in some places, but most of the time the vans are driving on dirt. It is a small town, much smaller than San Pablo.

The town looked very disorganized to Sammy, like it was put together hastily.

"I can never figure out where anything is in this town," Patti says. "The municipal hall is somewhere beside a school, I think. The hospital is somewhere up on a hill."

"Yvonne, you haven't been back here since you were what, about four years old, right?" Mari asks.

"Yeah, that's right," Yvonne says, looking intently out the window. "I don't remember this place," she whispers.

The vans park in a driveway beside a gas station.

Their brothers Robert, Morris and Marc are there to greet them.

"Where are we? This isn't the farm, is it?" Sammy asks.

"Oh no. You'll see it soon enough. Everyone is there waiting for you. Why don't you all get some refreshments?" Marc says, giving Lola a hand out of the van.

Robert leads the way to the back of the gas station. It is hot, but Sammy feels a breeze.

"Look," Vernon shouts. "We're right by the sea. Look at all those boats."

"There is barely any water where the boats are. Do they go anywhere?" Victoria asks.

"Duh, Victoria," Vernon says. "Have you never heard of low and high tides? You have to wait for the high tide and then the boats can go."

"How would I know that? We don't live by the water in California!" Victoria says, getting cranky.

"OK, enough. Go inside and have a soda or something," Mari says, pointing to the hut behind them.

A sign above the hut says Bayview.

"When we bought the gas station from our uncle, we got this as part of the bargain," Robert says.

There are tables and benches, a bar with stools and a kitchen in the back.

"High school kids like to come here for their *merienda* after school. People who live across the bay come to town by boat to go to market, and wait here for their ride back home. See those men in the straw hats squatting down there by the rocks? They own the boats. They make their living fishing or taking people across," Patti says.

"Who owns this, Tito Robert?" Sammy asks.

"Milly, Patti, Morris and myself. Morris and I pretty much run the place. We take turns managing it. When I'm in California, Morris runs the place and when he is in Canada, I run it," Robert says.

"Hey, look. A Karaoke machine with a big TV screen. Let's sing a few songs before leaving," Yvonne says, looking at the list of songs.

Sammy sees Ollie watching Yvonne.

Something was bothering your mom, Sammy. Did you notice she became really quiet when we drove through the town?

I noticed it too. Maybe it's because she is the only one who hasn't been here in so long. My aunts and uncles come here once a year. But my mom says this is her first time back since she was a child.

Lola walks through the doorway.

"Where is Yvonne? Be sure she is not by herself," Lola says worriedly.

"I'm right here, Mommy." Yvonne puts a token in the machine.

"This is for you, Sammy." Yvonne winks at her daughter, and belts out a song by the Beatles.

Everyone takes a turn at singing, but mostly Yvonne entertains them. Soon Morris comes in and says it's time to go. *Merienda* is being prepared at the farm.

Morris and Lola will ride with the vans. It is still the dry season so there are no problems with the dirt road.

"The rest of us are going to walk to the train station. Our transportation is waiting," Robert says.

"Are we going by train, Tito Robert?" Victoria asks.

"You'll see."

They walk toward the station, through the market stalls. The locals gawk at the newcomers. Yvonne and Jack take Sammy's hands and swing their daughter like they used to when she was little.

"You are getting a little too heavy for this. We used to be able to swing you higher," Yvonne says, laughing and panting slightly.

"What's this?" Sammy asks as they reach the station.

Lined up at the station are several motorized wooden sleds with rollers that scoot up and down the railroad track.

They remind her of the comical machines in the Bugs Bunny cartoons that she sees on TV on Saturday mornings. She has a vision of Bugs Bunny and Elmer Fudd pumping furiously, going down the railroad track.

"They're called skates here," Robert says.

"This is how we travel most of the time to the farm. It only takes about 15 or 20 minutes with stops along the way."

"Why do we have to stop?" Vernon asks.

PATRICIA LAUREL

"Depending on the load or how many passengers the skate is carrying, when you meet one of these, one gets off the track to let the one with the heavier load go on," Robert tells his nephew.

"What if a train is coming? You'll get flattened!" Vernon says.

"There are only two trains that come through here. One in the early morning and one late at night. Every skate driver knows the schedule," Robert says.

The skates have a couple of sturdy wooden planks for seats and a roof against the hot sun or pouring rain. The driver sits in the rear.

There are several skates lined up. Sammy and her parents get on the first one. Sammy is fascinated. She watches the driver pull on a string and the motor roars to life. He places his foot on a pedal; the skate lurches forward and sputters along the track.

They go pass ramshackle shacks and cement homes.

"Why do people live so close to the tracks?" Sammy asks.

"Squatters. They build on land that is not privately owned. This is considered government property," Robert says.

Ollie pats Sammy on the shoulder and points out a garbage filled creek running between the homes. It reeks so bad they hold their noses.

"Something needs to be done about that. What's happening in Manila shouldn't be happening here," Patti says.

The others nod. Sammy squeezes Ollie's hand. The adults are taking notice.

Their first stop is a busy intersection where other skates wait for passengers. There are stores and makeshift food stalls.

Everyone gets off. The driver and his helper balance the skate on their shoulders and lift it off the track. The group has a chance to have a quick look around. People greet the aunts and uncles.

Soon they board the skates and are on their way.

Sammy feels her pulse beating as they start again. She imagines she is on a safari to unknown parts, just like in adventure books.

The town and crowded stores are left behind. Sammy sees more open land.

Sammy has never seen so many coconut trees. There are fish hatcheries and rice fields in between, but mostly the huge leafy coconut trees that roll on forever. It is so beautiful.

"Welcome to the land of coconuts, Sammy," Patti says, "We're coming up to the edge of the farm. See those huts? That is where our land begins."

People come out of their homes waving. Down the track Sammy sees a little train station, where a small crowd has gathered.

PATRICIA LAUREL

"Are they waiting for us?" she asks.

"Yup. It's the welcoming committee. Look, there's Tito Mike," Yvonne points at her brother.

The skates screech to a rattling stop in front of the station. Mike waits for them along with some people Sammy does not know.

"Hey, you guys! Now that we're all here, the fiesta can officially begin," Mike says happily.

Luggage and boxes are unloaded from the skates. The skates are lifted from the tracks and placed neatly in a row by the train station.

Sammy and her cousins are introduced to some of Lolo's brothers and other cousins. Yvonne is reintroduced to relatives she hasn't seen since she left the country as a little girl.

To Sammy it looks like a very peaceful and quiet place, lush and green, just like in her dream.

She looks down the hill and sees several houses and a building with the Philippine flag.

"What is that building, Tito Mike?" she asks.

"That's the elementary school. The family built it after World War II for the children on the farm. Children from other villages attend school here as well."

"Who lives down in those houses?" Sammy asks.

"Marc has a house there along with some of our uncles, aunts, cousins and in particular the dreaded one," Patti laughs.

"Who is that?" Victoria asks.

"One of our cousins. I'm sure she'll make her entrance soon enough. Her name is Jenny. You need to watch out for that one," Patti says.

"Mom, is she mean?" Sammy asks.

"She visited with us before in San Francisco. You were so young, you probably don't remember. She stayed with us. I remember a few things that went missing after her visit. Never again!" Yvonne says.

"We tried to be nice to that one, but it didn't help," Mari says. "She will always be the conniving cousin."

"OK. Let's get you all settled. They're preparing a *merienda* and a get-together with the other relatives. Don't worry, you'll get your chance to meet the *bruha*. She's really scary!" Mike says, laughing and mussing the hair of one of his nieces.

"What's a *bruha*?" Sammy asks.

"A really mean witch that likes to gobble up little girls like you," Mike says, making a face. "But don't worry, I'll be here to protect you, Sam. Here, take my hand, just in case."

"Tito Mike, you're such a joker."

PATRICIA LAUREL

Sammy takes her uncle's hand. They start walking up to the houses, past the *barangay* or village hall. Mike explains that this is where the people gather when a meeting is called. This is also where the fiesta will be held.

There is a basketball court, a large open-air hall with a roof over it for shelter, a small day care center and a clinic. A few steps away is a small chapel.

A pathway from the chapel leads to Ika's house. The roof is thatched, similar to homes in the English countryside. It looks cozy and inviting. There is a hut next to it with screened windows. Ika says it is called the dirty kitchen. Cooking in the house is too hot and sticky.

Barking dogs race at them with their tails wagging furiously. Sammy notices one in particular. A huge black dog, the leader of the pack, bounds over to Ika.

"Prieto, my darling dog!" Ika says, with delight. Prieto jumps on his mistress and, with paws on her shoulders, starts licking her face.

"That's one big, beautiful, black dog," Yvonne says.

"Prieto is very friendly, but he can be seriously dangerous when threatened, or, if you try to give him a bath," Ika says. "He is a mixed Labrador, the best kind. Go on, you can pet him. He is like a lamb."

As if on cue, Prieto rolls on his back. Sammy rubs his tummy. He lies there content with huge paws in the air.

Chapter 11 ~ The Farm

After getting his fill of tummy rubbing, he gets up, looks at Sammy and gives her a huge lick on the face.

"Ick," Sammy says.

Ika laughs. "He likes you, Sammy. He does that to people he really likes."

"C'mon, let's get it together. Pretty soon it will be too late to eat *merienda*. Don't forget, there's still dinner after that," Mike says.

Sammy sees Milly up on the hill, waving from her house.

Sammy waves back.

There are several large tents spread out among the houses.

"What are those for?" she asks Patti.

"Well, you know there are so many of us. We've got tents set up outside large enough to house each family," Patti says.

"Where is Lola staying?" Sammy asks.

"She's staying at Ika's house, not so steep a climb for her," Mari says.

A new house sits halfway up the hill between Ika and Milly's homes. As they approach it, Sammy smells all the happy, fresh odors — sawn wood, paint and varnish.

It is a sprawling, one-level home with a bright, red tile roof and a wrap around screen porch. The porch hugs the house, makes it seem breezy, open and cool. There are big, screened windows all around.

A line of stepping-stones in the new yard winds through fruit trees and flowering plants. Big gold fish blow bubbles in a fishpond in the yard. Even the grass is new, springing up lime green in the freshly turned dirt.

"Wow, whose house is this?" Sammy says.

Jack grins at Yvonne. "I don't know," he says. "Let's go see if anyone is home."

They walk up onto the porch; their footsteps make a welcoming sound on the planks. The front door is open and Sammy peers inside. She sees a family room with a sofa, coffee table and wall hangings. At one end a large wooden table and straight-backed chairs make a dining area.

"Hello," Jack calls out. "Anyone home?"

Yvonne is laughing, "Oh, Jack," she says.

Suddenly Sammy knows, she jumps up and down, clapping her hands. "Oh, is it our house?" she says gleefully.

Jack smiles all the wider.

"It is our house," Sammy says. She quickly darts from room to room, exploring.

"Your mom and I built it together with Patti and John," Jack says.

Chapter 11 ~ The Farm

He and Yvonne hug each other.

A man and a woman come through the kitchen door. They are Daniel and Ligaya, the caretakers Patti hired. They used to work for Sammy's grandfather.

Daniel and Ligaya have lived on the farm all their lives. They knew each other as children, became sweethearts and married.

"I think I know them," Yvonne says to Patti.

"How could you? You haven't been here since you were a little girl. Patti and I know them," Mari says.

"Well, maybe. But something tells me that I know them. Maybe she was my *yaya*," Yvonne says.

"I used to watch you when you were this high," Ligaya says to Yvonne, holding a hand at her knee.

"See? I do know her and I remember liking them very much," Yvonne says to her sister. She puts her arm around Ligaya.

"They took care of Pappy until the very end. I wish he were here. He would be very happy to see all of us together," Mari says softly.

Patti puts a hand on her sister's shoulder. "That's why I asked Ligaya and Daniel to take care of the house. They live in a remote spot by the sea. Pappy gave them a plot of land as a wedding present."

"Sammy, this is a really cool house. Come out to the porch," Victoria says.

The porch is very inviting with ceiling fans whirling, rattan furniture with bright pillows and a hammock.

"Wow, you can see the ocean. Look, Victoria," Vernon says to his sister pointing at the blue South China Sea glistening on the horizon.

"Victoria! Come in here," her mother calls. "We've only been here a few minutes and already your things are scattered everywhere. I want you to pick them up right now."

Victoria lets out a big 'what a drag' sigh and goes inside. Sammy goes with her.

The cozy living room is filled with suitcases. There are three bedrooms that will be occupied by the adults.

"Where are we all going to sleep? The house isn't big enough," Victoria says.

"You girls will sleep on air mattresses out here in the living room. There is a large tent by the fish pond with sleeping cots for the boys," Mari says.

"It's like camping and a slumber party at the same time, huh Sammy?" Victoria says.

Sammy nods.

"OK. Put your stuff in our room and we'll organize everything later. I see Tita Ika coming," Mari says.

"Everyone is waiting for us at Tita Milly's."

Ika has to inspect the new house first. With her children and Prieto following, the eldest sister gushes over everything.

"Be sure to get the house blessed while you're here. It's really important. We don't want unwanted spirits floating around," she tells Patti.

"Ligaya is taking care of that. One day this week, the priest who comes here to say mass will do it," Patti replies.

"What do you mean by unwanted spirits floating around?" Sammy asks Ika.

"Oh, just superstition, but we're respecting a cultural belief shared by the local people. People will refuse to step foot in your house if it hasn't been blessed," Ika says.

"They have a lot of beliefs here. Right, mom?" Victoria says.

Mari nods.

Sammy notices that when Ollie is introduced to Ligaya, she holds on to Ollie's hand for a long time. Ollie does not seem to mind.

She goes outside with Victoria and Ollie to wait for the adults. Vernon goes to check out the tent he'll be sleeping in with his cousins. There is much to explore.

Daniel and Ligaya join the girls. Sammy sees the couple intently watching Ollie.

Ollie, Daniel and Ligaya seem to be really interested in you.

I know, but I feel comfortable around them.

Ollie looks at the couple. They nod and smile at her as if they understand mindtalk.

Hey Ollie, do you think they understand our mind talking?

They're not communicating with us, so they must not know how.

Ligaya approaches Ollie and gives her something. Delighted, Ollie thanks her and shows it to Sammy.

Sammy, guess what? Ligaya just gave me an anting-anting for protection. She said for me to wear it at all times, just like I told you when I gave you yours. She said that because this is a new place and I am stranger, I need protection from the bad spirits that live on the farm. She said it is better to be safe. Ligaya said she noticed you were wearing one, so she gave me hers.

What bad things could happen to us here? Sammy asks.

Victoria catches up with them. She saw Ligaya give Ollie the *anting-anting*.

"I want one of those. Do you think Ligaya can make me one?" she asks her mother, who has just emerged from the house.

Ligaya says something to Mari in Tagalog.

"Yes, she will make you one. Why is it you always want what others have? Be sure to thank Ligaya," Mari says.

Victoria gives Sammy and Ollie the — see I get one, too — look.

Sammy smiles at her cousin. Victoria can be a pain, but Sammy loves her. She takes her cousin's hand and they walk with Ollie up the hill to Milly's house.

Sammy sees it immediately. The towering mango tree, its branches heavy with fruit.

There. There it is. Just like in her dream.

The mound. She looks to see if she can see the figure she dreamed of. Where is it? Is the *BAWAL!* (FORBIDDEN!) sign there? Her eyes scan the area around the mound.

"Ouch! Sammy, let go of my hand! You're squeezing it too tight!" Victoria's protest breaks her concentration.

"Sammy, what's wrong?" Yvonne says, shaking her daughter gently while looking around her. She quickly leads her daughter away from the tree.

"Oh, Mom. I'm sorry, Victoria."

"It's OK. I guess your mind was somewhere else," Victoria says, rubbing her hand.

Ligaya says something to Yvonne.

Yvonne nods. Sammy can see that her mother has very much taken to Ligaya and Daniel.

"Ligaya says that sometimes there are snakes by the mango tree especially when the grass is high. She doesn't want us wandering over there. Daniel will take care of it tomorrow," she tells her daughter.

"OK, Mom."

Ollie has been quiet all this time, but Sammy can feel her friend is uneasy.

What is it, Ollie?

I don't like this feeling I have, Sammy. You must take care not go near that mound. I think something bad is there.

"C'mon you two! There's all kinds of food waiting for us and presents to give out to the relatives," Victoria says, running ahead.

They are greeted by more dogs, this time Milly's dogs. Like the other dogs down the hill, they all defer to Prieto.

"Prieto is the big boss dog," Patti says, laughing.

Everyone is gathered in Milly's outdoor dining hut. Lola sits in the midst of great-uncles, great-aunts and cousins who Sammy has never seen before. A lot of greeting and hugging go on. There are oohs and aahs when presents are brought out for Lolo's siblings. Sammy is swept up in the noisy, happy chatter.

Except for one woman fanning herself. She stands apart watching her aunts and uncles open their presents from the visiting relatives. She does not greet anyone. The others seem happy to leave her alone.

The woman turns her attention to Sammy. This must be the *bruha*. Oh no! She's coming this way.

Sammy looks around for Ollie, but she is being introduced to the relatives. Victoria is at the dining table, tasting the food. Daniel and Ligaya are helping in the kitchen.

The woman stares intently at Sammy as she approaches.

"Jenny, how are you? We haven't seen you in a while," Yvonne says.

With great relief, Sammy looks up to see her mother. Beside her are Patti and Milly.

"Sammy, this is Tita Jenny. She came to see us in San Francisco when you were just a little girl," Yvonne says.

Sammy does not remember Jenny. She takes hold of her mother's hand.

"So, this is your little girl," Jenny says, holding her hand out. "Hello, Sammy. You and I are going to get to know each other really well these next few days."

Sammy shakes her hand. It feels wet and clammy, like a fish. She wipes it on her shorts, hoping no one notices. Too late. Anger flashes in Jenny's eyes, but she recovers quickly.

Jenny pats Sammy on the head and makes small talk with her cousins. There is no warmth in the conversation.

PATRICIA LAUREL

"I just came up to welcome you to the farm. It is not often I see your family in this part of the world," Jenny says, smiling sweetly.

"That's so thoughtful of you, Jenny," Milly says, smiling sweetly in return.

"Well, enjoy yourselves. I'm off to town to run some errands," Jenny says.

They watch her leave, but not before she whispers something in Tito Joe's ear. Lolo's brother looks disturbed.

"She's up to no good," Patti says. "I'd keep an eye on her."

"Why did she single Sammy out?" Yvonne asks, with a worried look.

"It's OK, Mom," Sammy says. "I think it's because people were not paying any attention to her. I guess she came to me because she didn't have anybody to talk to."

"Maybe you're right, but I'd still watch out for her," Milly says. "Anyway, enough of Jenny. Let's eat!

[114]
Patricia Laurel

The Arbularyo

For the *merienda*, the long table holds all kinds of fruits, warm barbecued bananas and yams on spits, and *suman*, a sticky rice dish.

"C'mon Sammy. I'll teach you the proper way to eat a mango," Patti says.

She takes a whole mango and slices each side. "You can eat this with a spoon or take a knife and slice it lengthwise and crosswise, like so. Now you pick it up on each end and flip it. See, you have these mango cubes you can eat."

Mangoes are definitely at the top of Sammy's fave fruits list.

She also learns how to eat *suman*. Dip it in the wonderful tasting homemade cacao drink and then dip it in sugar. The taste is strange at first, but after a few more bites, Sammy decides she likes it. Not to mention the banana que — short for banana barbeque — with the sticky caramelized brown sugar. She's not too crazy about the barbequed yams.

Soon the table is cleared and the adults prepare to have a meeting about activities for the weeklong fiesta, which starts the next day. The older cousins will go to the courtyard to decorate it with banners and help set up the stage.

Some of the family will give a concert one night. They leave shortly after the *merienda* to rehearse.

Sammy and her cousins spend the next few hours helping set up the children's games and contests. Daniel and Ligaya, along with some of the *yayas*, are there to help.

Later, Milly asks would they like to see the lights go on the stage? The courtyard has been swept clean and there are colorful banners and lights all round. Booths are set up for the locals to sell food and drinks. The lights go on and everyone claps their hands in delight. All is in place.

After Mass the next morning, there will be a distribution of goods for the families who live on the farm after the blessing of the new house.

Sammy sees Daniel and Ligaya approach Lola. As a sign of respect, they take Lola's hand and put it to their foreheads. She does not recognize them, but after they tell her who they are, Lola sits down as if in shock. She looks around. Her gaze settles on Yvonne who is happily chatting with some of her siblings.

She says something to the couple with a worried look on her face. Ligaya takes Lola's hand as if to reassure her.

Sammy wonders what the secret is. She has much to write in her journal.

Soon it is time to go up the hill for dinner and an early bedtime. Tomorrow will be very busy.

Only the immediate family share the evening meal. The other relatives have gone back to their homes. After dinner, the family retreats to Milly's porch. It is the help's turn to eat.

Some of the aunts and uncles are with Morris inspecting his roosters. He shows them the fighting roosters that are being readied for the cockfights. The women in the family think it's barbaric and cruel, but know they can't stop it. It's a guy thing and there's nothing any of the aunts can do about it.

Sammy sits on the steps of Milly's porch, writing. She looks up and sees the mound beside the mango tree. Nothing there. Maybe she was just imagining things. Satisfied, she closes her journal.

The orange sun glows and fades and is replaced by inky night. Coming from a big city, Sammy has never seen such black sky sprinkled with so many big, glittering stars. She hears what sounds like billions of crickets and frogs. The porch lights come on.

Milly sits in a rocking chair. She and Sammy are the only ones on the porch. She suddenly bends over, grasping her stomach.

"Aiiiiiiiiieeeeeeeee!!!"

"What's wrong, Tita Milly?" Sammy jumps up.

"Sweetie, go get Tito Ron. Tell him I am having terrible stomach pains," she says, wincing.

Sammy runs to where Milly's husband, Ron, is talking with the other uncles.

"Tito Ron! Come quickly! There is something wrong with Tita Milly!"

Everyone rushes to the porch. Milly clutches her stomach and struggles to get up from the rocking chair. Ron takes her into their bedroom. He puts his wife gently onto the bed.

"What is wrong?" Ika asks.

Milly doubles up in pain. "I've got really bad stomach cramps."

Ika touches her forehead. Milly is burning up and her skin feels clammy.

"What are we going to do? It's already dark and our uncle who is the only doctor anywhere for miles doesn't arrive from Manila until tomorrow," Ika says.

Milly's housekeeper says something to Morris. He nods.

"The only thing we can do is to send for the *arbularyo*. She is the only healer on the farm, but she lives by the beach and it will take at least a couple of hours to get there and back," Morris says.

Several horses are saddled. There are reluctant volunteers among the locals. One of the wives of the men picked to go says something and clutches the *anting-anting* around her neck.

Sammy sees that many of them are wearing charms, around their necks or wrists.

"I'd forgotten how superstitious this lot can be," Morris says. "They think the *engkantos* are out and about." He sniffs. "Enchanted creatures!"

One of the men says something that makes Marc laugh.

"My friend here says that if the big Americanos go with us, then they'll go. Maybe the *engkantos* will be afraid of them because of their size."

"OK. Jack, Ron and I will go. We'll protect you guys," John says, growling and puffing his chest.

Just as the men are about to leave, Daniel runs up.

"What luck! The *arbularyo* and her granddaughter are staying with Daniel and Ligaya for the fiesta. They just arrived," Robert says.

A collective sigh of relief goes up, especially from the locals. Even Sammy's father and uncles, who do not believe in superstitions, seem more relaxed.

Ligaya approaches with a girl and an old woman who walks with a cane.

The old woman is Nanay Gustia and the girl is her granddaughter, Eva. Ligaya says that during the fiesta Nanay Gustia sits at the courtyard and sells her medicinal herbs and gives advice to the locals. Since most of the people are cash poor, she usually receives food for her services.

They live in a small hut on the family's beachfront property. Lolo gave them the land, just as he did for Daniel and Ligaya. Sammy wishes she had known her grandfather. From what she's heard, everyone loved and respected him.

"Yikes! What is that on her shoulder?" Victoria shrieks, grabs Sammy and points at Nanay Gustia.

"Don't point," Sammy scolds her cousin. "It's not polite."

"But look!" Victoria says, drawing back and getting behind Sammy. "What is that thing?"

Perched on Nanay Gustia's right shoulder is a huge, albino gecko. Its skin is the color of milk with large liver-colored spots. The gecko has bright pink eyes, a red mouth and a long, scaly tail. It twists its old head from side to side, peering this way and that, taking everything in.

In the dim moonlight, the gecko appears to glow in the dark.

Nanay Gustia acts as if she doesn't even know it's there.

"Wow!" says Vernon. "That old lizard on her shoulder is as big as a loaf of bread."

"Ugh," the girls say.

"It's bigger than a football," Vernon says excitedly. "I'll bet it eats huge bugs. Tito Morris, do you think we could get one?"

Morris laughs.

As they draw closer, the gecko arches its back like a cat and hisses.

The kids all shrink back, including Vernon, whose enthusiasm quickly fades. The old woman jabbers at them and pets her lizard, soothing it.

"Nanay Gustia says that her gecko is not used to being around so many people," Morris says.

The two are led toward the house where Lola waits for them. Sammy hears Eva say *mano po*, taking Lola's hand and placing it on her forehead, just like Ligaya and Daniel. Lola takes Nanay Gustia's hands in greeting.

Eva takes the gecko from her grandmother and puts it on her shoulder. She stays on the porch while the old woman goes inside the house where the aunts are waiting. Lola and the others remain outside.

The other kids are interested in the gecko, but Sammy is more curious about Nanay Gustia's method of healing. She slips inside.

Milly lies on the bed with her sisters standing around her. Nanay Gustia asks about her pain and what she had eaten. Turns out Milly has been munching on sweets all day long and being so busy with the fiesta preparations, she forgot to eat a proper meal. Plus, she picked a very green, sour mango from the tree, and ate it with salt.

Sammy follows Nanay Gustia into the kitchen. She produces a small cloth bag and takes out a handful of herbs.

She asks Milly's housekeeper to boil water and for a mortar and pestle. She brews what looks like green tea.

"I want to know what she's doing and what kind of stuff she is using!" Milly hollers in panic.

Nanay Gustia squats on the floor and examines more of her herbs. She takes a dark brown oval-shaped nut, bites a piece from it and starts chewing. Then she takes a mixture of herbs and grinds it in the pestle. She puts the ground up herbs in her hand and spits in what she was chewing. The spit is reddish. She mixes everything with a finger.

She looks up at Sammy and smiles. She has red stains around her mouth and in between her teeth.

"Yuck!" Sammy says, covering her mouth.

"What?" Milly croaks from the bedroom.

The sisters rush to the kitchen. They look at Nanay Gustia's concoction and return to Milly.

"What did Sammy find so disgusting?" Milly asks anxiously.

"Oh, Sammy's not used to seeing this type of healing. It's all new to her, right?" Yvonne says to her daughter with raised eyebrows.

"That's right, Tita Milly. I've never seen medicine like that before," Sammy says.

Nanay Gustia comes into the room with one hand cupped.

Patricia Laurel

Milly winces. "I don't like the looks of whatever that is."

"Oh, don't worry about it. It's perfectly safe. It won't poison you. Nanay Gustia hasn't killed anyone yet with her herbs," Ika says.

The old woman rubs the potion on Milly's forehead and stomach. The greenish brown concoction looks slimy. The smell is awful. Milly makes gagging sounds. Nanay Gustia rubs more of the stuff on Milly's tummy.

Sammy looks at her mother and aunts. She sees Patti and Mari with their faces buried in their hands and shoulders shaking. Are they crying? Do they think their sister is about to die?

She looks at Ika and her mother. They are choking back laughter. Patti has tears streaming down her face. Finally, they all howl.

Milly drinks Nanay Gustia's brew and makes a face. "It is not funny, you guys!"

"Sorry, Milly," Patti says, wiping the tears from her face. "How are you feeling?"

"Better. Amazingly enough."

"OK, let's call it a night. Hope you're feeling better, sis," Mari says.

"Not until I wash this stuff off me," Milly says, and stumbles into the bathroom.

They go outside where the others are waiting. Yvonne tells them what happened. The sisters start laughing all over again.

"Anyway, Milly feels better," Yvonne says.

Sammy watches Nanay Gustia and Eva sitting together. The gecko is back on the old woman's shoulder. Eva pulls her long hair back. Behind the ear is a blue slit, like a small mouth.

Despite her amazement, Sammy doesn't say a word.

It dawns on Sammy. "Eva is the girl swimming in the ocean in my dream."

Eva pats her hair back in place. Sammy tries not to stare.

Soon they all take their leave and head back down the hill. Soft yellow lights glow in the tents where the others get ready for bed. Sammy sees their shadows against the white canvas.

She looks back to see Lola walking with Ligaya, Daniel, Nanay Gustia and Eva. Lola seems to be giving them instructions.

Sammy reaches out to Ollie.

Ollie, there are secrets here that we don't know about.

Yes. I can feel it. I think it has something to do with your mother.

Ligaya and Daniel are staring at her and Ollie, but quickly look away when they catch Sammy and Ollie staring at them. Sammy feels they know what she and Ollie are saying.

"This place is a lot of fun, huh Sammy?" Victoria says, catching up with them.

"Yes it is. I can't wait. The fiesta goes on for a whole week," Sammy says.

Everyone kisses Lola good night. Lola puts her hand on her eldest daughter's arm for support and together they walk down to Ika's house.

Goodnight, Ollie.

Goodnight, Sammy. Sleep well.

Larry comes out of the bathroom when they enter the house. "OK. The bathroom is yours. We're all done. Good night," he says, walking out.

Victoria leaps onto the air mattress that has been set out in the living room. It slides on the tiled floor and bumps into the sofa.

"Cool. Is this where Sammy and I are sleeping?"

"Victoria! Stop messing around and get ready for bed," Mari says.

"You too, Sammy," Yvonne says.

"Moms can be a drag, don't you think?" Victoria whispers.

Soon the house is quiet. Sammy writes in her journal before she turns off the light. She puts a check mark beside

Nanay Gustia and Eva's names. She is sure they were in her dream.

Could Daniel and Ligaya be the man and woman who were standing on the beach beside Nanay Gustia? She puts question marks by their names.

She lies next to Victoria on the air mattress. Her cousin is in Zee Land, as Tito John calls it.

Sammy listens to the night creatures. She hears the sounds of geckos hunting for bugs, crickets and an army of frogs.

She senses movement out on the porch. Her heart beats a little faster. Who is out there? She gets up and looks out the window.

Nanay Gustia sits erect in a chair, walking cane on her lap, as if she were guarding the house. She sees Sammy from the window and says, "*Tulog na*."

Sammy whispers, "OK." She knows Nanay Gustia is telling her to sleep.

Her uneasiness slips away. She lies back down and closes her eyes. Like Victoria beside her, she drifts off to Zee Land.

The Fiesta

"Sammy, it's time to get up." She likes to hear her mother's gentle voice waking her. Victoria would have shouted in her ear.

She begins her waking up ritual with a few yawns and stretches before giving her mother a good morning hug.

"Good morning, Sammy," Ligaya says, when Sammy walks into the kitchen.

"*Magandang umaga*," Sammy replies in Tagalog. She can tell Ligaya is pleased to hear a child born and raised elsewhere, speak her mother's language.

She and her parents go to Milly's for breakfast.

"What's on the agenda today?" Jack asks Larry.

"As soon as we get done eating here, the *cucineros* we hired will take over and prepare lunch for the people. A priest from town will say Mass, and I think he will also bless your house. After that, we distribute presents."

Sammy sees a group of men and women squatting on the ground with plates in one hand, eating with the other. There are a few pigs with ropes around their necks and many baskets of clucking chickens.

Sammy sloppily mimics their style of eating. She hears Milly laughing behind her. She looks much better than she did the night before.

PATRICIA LAUREL

"Would you like to learn to eat with your hands, Sammy?"

"I'm not doing a very good job."

"I know what we'll do. When we go on our annual beach picnic, I'll have banana leaves spread out on the picnic table with no plates and silverware. We'll flop the food on the leaves and you can make a mess. What do you think?"

"We're going to the beach?"

"Yes, we'll have loads of fun. We used to go on picnics to the beach all the time."

"Is everyone going, Tita Milly?"

"I think so. It's a tradition during fiesta. We always save one day for a beach trip…oops, gotta go, Sam. Looks like they're starting to set up."

People quickly get busy. In the yard, vegetables, fruits, large metal basins and cooking utensils are on a long table. A large pot of water boils on a brick oven. The squealing pigs have been tied to the posts and the chickens in the covered basket are placed on the floor.

Ligaya, Nanay Gustia and Eva are busy in the dirty kitchen, slicing vegetables. Daniel helps the *cucineros*.

Sammy sees her cousins climbing the hill.

"Sammy, are you going to watch what they do to the pigs and the chickens before cooking them?" Vernon asks.

"I don't think so. I'm going back to the house," Sammy says, making a face.

"Where is Ollie?" Sammy asks.

"She went into town with Tita Ika to get supplies. They'll be back before lunch," Vernon says.

Soon the rest of the clan joins them.

"Looks like they need help holding down the pigs," Robert says.

"C'mon, Sammy. Let's go see what they're doing," Victoria says, dragging her.

The noise from the animals increases, as if they know what awaits them. Sammy covers her ears. A squirming pig is being held down. It is too much for Sammy.

Milly comes out with a bottle of brandy. "Here, see if this will help. Give it some of this and maybe it will calm down," she says, handing the bottle to Mike.

It seems everyone's attention is on the poor animal. Sammy decides now is a good time to flee. No one notices.

She runs back to their house and looks into her parents' bedroom. Jack is asleep on the bed with a book on his chest. There is no one else in the house.

She can still hear the pitiful squeals of the animals, but not as bad. Sighing, she takes her journal and goes out to the porch. Her quiet time does not last long. From the corner of her eye, she sees a figure moving towards her. It's that strange aunt she met yesterday.

PATRICIA LAUREL

Sammy remembers Patti's words describing her. "She is a female version of Uriah Heep. She slinks around and gets into your good graces and Bam! You won't know what hit you."

"Who is Uriah Heep?" Sammy had asked.

"You have to read *David Copperfield*. Heep is positively eeky and slimy."

Sammy writes a reminder in her journal to read *David Copperfield*. She and her aunt share the same taste in books.

She remembers asking her dad a question about books when she was about 5 years old.

"Dad, what happens to words when you close a book?"

Jack, ever ready with an answer says, "Oh, they visit each other, chat and drink tea. Later, they have to make sure they're back in order."

Sammy liked that answer a lot.

"What are you doing, Sammy?" Jenny asks.

Tita Patti is right. She does sort of slink…like a snake.

"Oh, nothing. Just writing down a few things in my journal."

Should have kept quiet about that, too late. Sammy thinks to herself as she snaps the plastic case of her journal shut.

Sammy hears another loud gurgling squeal from up the hill and puts her hands over her ears.

Jenny smiles at her.

"Why are you here by yourself? Don't you want to see the *cucineros* do their work?" Jenny asks, staring with interest at the journal in its bright plastic case.

Sammy returns the journal to her backpack.

"No, thanks. I'm not alone. My dad is inside reading." She feels safer saying that Jack is around.

This does not seem to faze Jenny. She sits down in front of Sammy.

Sammy feels butterflies in her stomach. Not the hunger kind of fluttering in her tummy, but the kind that signals to be alert and take care.

Jenny has a bag with her. She fishes inside and brings out what looks like little balls in colorful plastic wrappers. "Here, take some. These are my favorite sweets in the whole world."

Trying to be polite, Sammy takes one and unwraps it. The sweet treat is sticky with caramel glaze. It almost reminds her of Marie-Jean's cream puffs.

Sammy bites into it. The center is creamy and soft. The taste is nowhere near her beloved cream puffs, but it is tasty.

"They're called *yemas*," Jenny says, thinking that this was going to be easy.

Sammy takes another piece of *yemas*, smiling at Jenny. The warning signals are getting louder.

"Do you like it here on the farm?" Jenny asks.

Sammy nods vigorously, munching away.

Jenny chatters on, while Sammy wishes she would go away.

"Huh?" she asks when she feels Jenny tugging at her sleeve. She suddenly finds Jenny sitting next to her. Sammy moves to the edge of the couch. A flash of anger shows on Jenny's face, and just as quickly vanishes.

Sammy can sense it's a real effort for Jenny to be nice.

"Your mind seems to be elsewhere. I was telling you about my favorite mango tree. It's one of the largest ones in the province. And its fruit is delicious. Do you want me to show you?"

"I shouldn't. My mom will wonder where I am. I'm supposed to tell her where I am at all times. Maybe when she gets back, we can go with you."

"Oh no, it's not far at all. Look, it's right over there," Jenny says, pointing to the mango tree.

The shady tree is very alluring. She gazes at it and wonders why she was afraid of it yesterday. From where she is sitting, it looks harmless.

She gets up and walks with Jenny toward the tree mesmerized, as if a large invisible magnet is pulling her.

A few more steps and she is almost there. She feels her head getting heavier.

"SAMMEE!" a shout breaks the spell.

Sammy turns to see Nanay Gustia waving and Eva running to her.

If looks could strike you down, Jenny's glare would have finished the old woman and her granddaughter.

"What are you doing here? Leave us alone!" she screeches. But it is too late.

"Your mama, she wants you," says Eva in halting English, urgently beckoning to Sammy.

Sammy runs to them. She feels herself breaking away from something invisible and powerful.

Jenny composes herself, and says, "Oh well, maybe next time."

She gives Sammy the sweetest smile she can muster, but darts a look of hatred at the other two. Jenny starts down the hill, furiously fanning herself.

As if waking from a bad dream, Sammy shakes herself and looks at Nanay Gustia and Eva.

"Wow, *salamat po*," she says, thanking her rescuers.

Nanay Gustia and Eva are on either side of her as they walk to Milly's porch.

Sammy turns around and looks at the mango tree and the mound beside it. Is it her imagination or is the mound trembling? She turns away, shuddering.

The squealing of the pigs has stopped. Pretty soon her cousins join her. Victoria tells Sammy that Tito Morris had the *cucineros* hold down each pig as he poured a shot of brandy down its throat. It seemed to work, because the pigs were calmer.

"So, what did you do with yourself?" Victoria asks.

"Oh, not too much. Just wrote a little in my journal."

Something's happened. I can feel it, Ollie says from behind her. She and Ika have just returned from town. Sammy tells her what happened.

Sammy, stay away from Jenny. She is a very dangerous person. I feel she is up to no good.

I can sense her hatred for my family. I think she means to hurt us.

Don't worry. I am sure there are people here looking out for you and the family.

Victoria interrupts their mind talk.

"C'mon Sam. We're going down to watch the basketball game between our uncles and the workers. And then Lola promised to tell us family stories after siesta."

Sammy is delighted. She loves Lola's stories. She forgets about Jenny.

She joins her parents as they walk to the courtyard. "Did you have a nice nap, Dad?"

"Yes, I did. I never nap after breakfast. But the bed looked so inviting and I didn't want to watch the slaughter of the animals."

"Sammy, don't go wandering off by yourself, OK? Be sure someone is always with you," Yvonne says.

Sammy holds their hands. "OK, mom."

They spend the morning cheering on the men of the family who are on the losing side of the basketball game.

Further down the hill, all is quiet. Everyone scatters when they see Jenny storm inside her bungalow. People avoid her black moods. She fumes and fans herself.

The cheers of her hated relatives do nothing to help her mood. "That will change soon!" she mutters angrily.

She goes out on the patio. She stares across the railroad tracks, up the hill at her cousins' houses. She thinks about how she will tear the houses down as soon as she takes possession of the farm.

"You did not come through for me!" a voice says behind her.

Jenny jumps from her chair.

PATRICIA LAUREL

"How dare you sneak up on me!" Jenny shrieks, touching her forehead. It feels like a piercing migraine attack.

The *duwende* bows mockingly. "Did we startle Her Highness? We beg her forgiveness."

"What did you do to me? My head is on fire! Stop it this instant!"

"Did you forget that I placed that mark there so you can focus on your job?"

He waves his cutlass and Jenny's excruciating pain vanishes. She staggers to the chair.

"That was just the first attempt. I'm still testing the waters, so to speak. Don't you worry your little self. I have a whole week," Jenny laughs at her smart remark.

"See that you do or the our deal is off ... more than that."

"What do you mean by that? You'll turn me into a wart?"

The *duwende* chuckles threateningly. "Do your job and remember our bargain. The girl in exchange for the riches you dream of."

"All right. Let me do it my way and no more headaches!" Jenny touches her forehead. Is it her imagination or does the mark feel a little lumpy?

The *duwende* disappears before she can say more.

Jenny goes back inside, lies on the sofa and contemplates her next move. The girl is on her guard now. She thinks

Chapter 13 ~ The Fiesta

about the pesky old woman and her granddaughter. She will make them pay, all of them.

Something nags at her. The *duwende*. She is not sure their deal is to her liking. Deep inside she knows not only Sammy, but she too, is in danger of coming under that creature's enchantment.

She will take the risk. "I'll have to think of something," she murmurs. Soon she is asleep, dreaming of riches.

PATRICIA LAUREL

14

Lolo

After the basketball game, the people are treated to a hearty lunch in the hall by the courtyard. The family serves up the portions. Sammy and her cousins are assigned to the beverage and dessert table. After the meal, presents are distributed.

"The fiesta is really all about the people. Without them, we would not be able to run the farm," Robert says.

After the presents are distributed, they head towards the new house for the blessing.

Sammy watches the priest say his prayers and sprinkle holy water in every room as well as the outside grounds. Her attention turns to Nanay Gustia. The old woman's head is covered with a towel, knotted on top of her head to hold it in place. She is careful not to draw attention to herself and lingers behind the group.

Sammy follows Nanay Gustia and watches her perform her ritual of protection against evil spirits. She holds a candle, and takes out herbs from her cloth bag hanging from a belt on her waist. She whispers to herself, strews her blend of herbs all over and bows her head several times. She is chewing that disgusting red nut that turns her teeth red.

Her own blessing performed, Nanay Gustia walks outside the house where the others are talking to the priest. Sammy sees

Patricia Laurel

the priest give Nanay Gustia a disapproving look, but he does not say anything. It's useless to try and change the old ways.

The family climb up the hill to Milly's for their meal. Any signs of the *cucineros'* work are all gone except for the large freezer chest humming beside the dirty kitchen.

The smells from the kitchen are heavenly and make Sammy's mouth water.

After a meal of chicken and pork adobo, fried fish, fried rice and mango for dessert, comes the clattering clank of people cleaning up after a feast. It is the quiet time, when the sun is hottest and no one moves. *Siesta* time.

Lola says she must rest her eyes. Sammy goes with her to their newly blessed house. They pass John napping in the hammock by the fishpond.

When they reach the house, Sammy follows Lola into one of the bedrooms.

"Sammy, come and lie down beside me and tell me what you've been up to. Do you like it here?"

"Very much, Lola. It's very beautiful and peaceful. I would like to come here more often."

She tells Lola about school, her projects and friends. Something tells her to leave out the dream, her gift of mind talk and the strange things that have happened to her. It might upset her grandmother. She does talk about the instant connection she and Solo made, but not about the images on the moon and Solo's warning to careful.

Lola listens intently. "Solo must be just like you. You both feel and see things that others can't. Are you sure there is nothing else you want to tell me?"

"No, Lola. But you know what? Tita Patti has a little bit of mind…" Sammy stops herself.

"That's good, Sammy. Don't worry. Lola will look out for you and your mother," Lola's eyes close.

"Why should anything happen to me or mom?" Sammy asks, but Lola does not answer.

Sammy yawns and soon drifts away.

Lola lies beside her granddaughter with eyes closed. She should be more careful. Why alarm the child? It all happened so long ago.

Soon she too drifts off to sleep, thinking of her husband. I would feel so much better if you were here. We would all be safe…"

The man carries a bundle wrapped in a blanket. He gets off his horse and hands the reins to Morris. "Be careful, hijo. You and Gustia finish up here and follow me as soon as you can," he says to his son who gives him a parting embrace.

He pets the horse and whispers in its ears, as if to assure it that he will come back. He turns around to see the last glimmer of light disappear among the trees. The light that guided them in the dark.

He walks over to three figures standing by the banca. One carries a lantern, the only light in the black night. The waves lap against the boat as he and the two others climb in. Gustia stays behind with Morris. No one speaks.

He sighs with relief once they pull away from shore. He feels movement from the bundle in his arms. He peeks inside the blanket. The little girl is asleep. He looks at the peaceful face and hugs her close to him.

"Don't worry, hija. Pappy will take you where it is safe," he murmurs to his sleeping daughter.

He knows they are still in danger of being found. The man is not afraid for himself. It's his youngest daughter this thing is after. His other children are safe with their mother in San Pablo. The older girls are in Madrid. His wife had made arrangements for her and the rest of the children to leave for America.

There are other reasons for his family to get away. Martial Law has been declared by a ruthless man in control of the government. Many relatives and friends have made plans to leave. Only he will stay behind. Someone has to stay and manage the farm.

He stares at the water with a great sadness. How did it come to this? A greedy politician splitting his family apart, and a dark creature of the earth trying to steal his daughter.

He heard the stories from his people. He knows of children who have gone missing from the farm.

He strains his neck to see the disappearing forms of Gustia and his eldest son on the beach. If she had not intercepted the creature, his daughter Yvonne would be lost forever.

The other two on the boat are Ligaya and Daniel. He should be angry with them for being careless with Yvonne and letting her wander off, but kids are kids. The teenagers have been inseparable since they were children. I wouldn't be surprised if they end up married, he thinks to himself.

These two and Gustia are his most loyal and trusted people.

"Kuya Bobby," Daniel taps him respectfully on the shoulder. They have reached the rocky shore of the town. They get out and climb the stony steps to his brother's Cafe. The Cafe is closed and no one is about.

They rush to his jeep. He hands his sleeping daughter to Ligaya and starts the engine. It is a long drive to San Pablo.

His wife is waiting when they arrive. Little Yvonne is taken upstairs. "Do not leave her alone for one minute," he tells Ligaya.

He and his wife go into the living room to discuss what lies ahead.

"You can come with us, Bobby," she says.

"We've been through this. Someone has to stay here or our lands will be lost. Maybe when things calm down, I can come for a visit," he says, knowing deep down that it won't happen.

The next morning he drives his wife and children to the airport. The children cling to their father, afraid of letting him go. It is time to say goodbye.

He hugs his children fiercely and tells them to take care of each other and respect and love their mother. Now they are crying, not understanding why their father must stay behind.

They stand there at the lounge, reluctant to move. He says to his wife, "Go, now."

He watches them head for the gate. His wife turns around. He nods at her and waves. She holds Yvonne's hand. And she and the children are gone.

His heart aches as he walks back to the parking lot where Daniel and Ligaya wait. For the first time since the war that took so many lives, he hangs his head and weeps.

PATRICIA LAUREL

15

Stories

Sammy wakes up alone.

It must be mid afternoon. Back in the States, everyone is on a schedule. Here on the farm, it is as if time does not matter. "I come here to be revived" Patti says. "Here, time has no meaning for me, at least for a little while."

Sammy goes into the living room. Victoria sleeps on the sofa, her eyeglasses hanging crookedly on her nose. Sammy removes the glasses and puts them on the coffee table.

She hears movement outside. Lola sits on the porch in a rocking chair, deep in thought. She does not see her granddaughter until Sammy stands in front of her.

"Did you have a good nap?" she asks.

"Yes, I did. Lola, are you all right? You seem to be worried about something."

"Oh, it's nothing. I'm just thinking of the past and your Lolo."

Sammy feels that there is something else. She wishes her grandmother would tell her. Maybe she could help.

"It looks like siesta time is over. Everyone's gathering," Lola says. Sammy sees relief in Lola's eyes at the interruption.

Her aunts and cousins gather on the porch. Except for Robert who hates to miss out on family stories, the men are busy preparing for the evening's festivities.

Victoria wakes up. "What's for *merienda*?" she asks, rubbing the sleep from her eyes.

As if on cue, Ligaya brings out a platter of barbequed bananas and yams. Nanay Gustia comes out followed by Eva with two pitchers of cold cantaloupe and mango juices.

After satisfying their appetites, Sammy and Ollie sit on the floor with the rest of the cousins and aunts.

"Lola, please tell us about our Chinese ancestor," Sammy says. The other kids groan and the grownups smile patiently, having heard it all before. But Sammy has her journal open and her pen in hand.

Vernon pushes his eyes at a slant and makes a silly grin, but Mari smacks her son lightly on the back of the head. "Behave, Vernon," she says.

"Our family patriach was the merchant Cue Yi-Lam," Lola says. "He came from the Fujian province in the south of China, from a village called Siongque. Its name means City of Spring. He was the 19th generation of the first Chou to settle there. The family line can be traced back 3,000 years to the Chou Dynasty."

Sammy writes away, taking it all down. Lola smiles approvingly.

"The Spanish," Lola says, "who were not known for their tolerance, had a great prejudice toward the Chinese people. They made them pay higher taxes and persecuted them in many ways.

"So our ancestor changed his name to Domingo Lamco." She held her finger up for emphasis.

"Still the Spanish were not satisfied, he took on the name of Mercado, which means market in Spanish, so his descendants would not forget their Chinese merchant roots. He was even baptized in the Catholic faith in the Chinese ghetto of Manila — Domingo Lamco Mercado.

"He moved to Biñan, Laguna and married a Chinese *mestiza*. Eventually, our side of the family relocated to the nearby town of Calamba. They built the first stone house, owned the first piano ever seen in the province, the first carriage and a flour mill," Lola says, finishing the story of their ancestor's emigration to the Philippines.

"Thank you, Lola," Sammy says, closing her journal.

"I hope you're not going to write all of Lola's stories in your journal," Victoria says to her cousin. "We'll be here forever with your questions!"

"Maybe not all," Sammy says.

Victoria groans.

[150]
PATRICIA LAUREL

16

The Plot Thickens...

Down the hill from the train station, a man sits on his patio. Joe was once the strongest man for miles around. He stood tall in the province, tall like a tree. When he was young and hale, Joe was all muscle and strength, had a booming voice and a loud laugh. But now he is getting old and things aren't going his way.

Two boys, children of the farm workers, walk up smiling. They wear shorts, T-shirts and rubber slippers. Each holds a brightly painted matchbox with his name written on it in red. They hold the boxes up before him.

"Kuya Joe," one of the boys says with a gap-toothed grin, "you like to see them fight today?"

"Why not?" Joe says, jingling a few coins.

The boys open the matchboxes and each pulls out a large black spider. They hold them up for Joe's inspection.

"Well," Joe says, "they seem most ferocious."

The spiders gingerly wave their long, crooked legs. The boys hold them closer together, and they become more agitated.

"I pick this fellow," Joe says. "What's his name?"

"Joker," the boy says happily. "He's a fighter, Kuya Joe."

The boys put the spiders on a long stick and hold it between them. At first the spiders are cautious, feeling one another out, feinting, testing. Then they have at it, flicking out tiny gossamer strands, trying to snare one another. It's as if they are fencing.

Soon, Joker is in trouble. Once he is helplessly entangled, the other spider moves in for the kill, and begins to devour his victim.

"Aww, Joker," the gap-toothed boy says mournfully.

The other boy holds out his palm expectantly and Joe hands over a few more coins.

"Let that be a lesson to you, boys," Joe says. "Nobody wins them all."

Joe watches them go on their way and tries to remember what it was like to be a child, with no cares, no worries. The memory eludes him.

He rocks back and forth, hands covering his face.

His name is Jose, but his family and friends call him Joe. He is one of Lolo's brothers. Joe married late in life and has five young children to care for.

"I was only thinking of my children's future," he whispers miserably.

Joe borrowed a large amount of money from the bank using his properties as collateral to invest in what he thought was a sure deal. But the investment was a scam and his partners vanished.

He is dead broke. Now the bank bangs on his door and he has no money to pay. He is too ashamed to approach his brothers and sisters.

Suddenly the sky turns black. He looks up. It is a cloud of fruit bats, with their big black wings whooshing eerily. This time of day, a bad sign. Sunset is the time for fruit bats.

"Just what I need. Another bad omen," he mutters.

"And here comes more trouble." He groans as he sees his niece Jenny coming toward him.

"What's wrong, Tito Joe? You look like you've lost something very precious. Is there anything I can do to help?" Jenny asks sweetly.

"You said you wanted to talk to me about something, Jenny. What is it?"

"I'll get straight to the point, dear uncle. I've heard you sank a lot of money in a bad investment."

"Do you make it a habit to look into other people's finances?"

Jenny ignores his question. "I have a proposition that will make you financially secure for the rest of your life. That is, if you succeed."

"What is it?"

"I took it upon myself to take over your loan. The bank will not be hounding you, but I will. All I want from you is one teensy-weensy favor."

Joe stares at Jenny and moans. "This cannot be good."

"If you succeed, I will forgive your loan plus you will receive a very fat bonus. Your problems will all be behind you. If you don't come through for me, I will turn you and your family out and take over your remaining assets."

"So, what is this teensy-weensy favor?" He knows he has no choice.

Jenny tells her uncle that through her business contacts, she has learned that the country's largest electric company wants an ocean site property for a power plant. She made inquiries and found out that the family's farm fits all the requirements, so she made an offer to the company, of course, without consulting the family first.

Now the company has accepted. "They have agreed to pay a sum of money that you and I can only dream of, Tito!"

Several hundred acres of the family's beachfront will be required. A road will be built from the farm's compound to the beach for hauling heavy equipment and machines.

All she has to do is produce the title with everyone's signature and the sale can go through.

Joe looks around him while his niece chatters away about all the riches to be gained.

He likes the peaceful, clean air and simple country living. He was raised here. Except for when he was educated in Manila, this is where he has spent his life. He looks at the huge cross up on the hill where his parents and siblings rest in peace.

He imagines the peace being shattered with heavy trucks and equipment, the air infested with black smoke and the quiet solitude broken by the sounds of roaring machines. The only noise now is the occasional whistle of the train.

Is he willing to give this up? Does he have a choice?

"Tito! Are you listening to me?" Jenny's screeching voice hurts his ear.

Joe rubs his ear. "I don't see how you can convince the rest of the family to go along with this insanity. You know that not one of them will agree to it! You will never pull it off!"

"You let me worry about that. That is my department."

"What do you need me for?"

"I want you to do a couple of things. First, be my eyes and ears. I need to know what Tita Marita's family is up to at all times. I tried, but they do not trust me. And I need you to get Yvonne's daughter Sammy to the mango tree. Be sure she is alone. I don't want any meddlers around when it happens."

"When what happens? Why do you want Sammy near the tree?"

Joe's eyes are bulging. He remembers the stories.

The tree has always been there. As a young boy, he was told to steer clear of it. Bad things were bound to happen, especially to children. He never let his own go near it.

"Oh no! I'm not going to do your dirty deed for you. Sammy is just a child. Where is your conscience?"

Jenny's smoldering anger flows to the surface like lava. He imagines her face turning a vicious purple-red, ready to explode. Joe has never seen anyone full of hate. He moves away from Jenny, as if afraid of burning himself. It scares him.

"What have they done to you that is so awful? They are good people and do not deserve the pain and misery you are about to inflict on them. On all of us."

He expects her to shriek at him again and prepares to cover his ears. Instead, her words are composed and cold, sending a shiver down Joe's spine.

"I have endured their tolerance and pity for too long. All of you. Even you, Tito Joe. You have all been against me ever since I can remember, and don't think I don't know what is being said about me behind my back. I will never be a part of this family. It is time I pay every one back for everything I've had to put up with.

"But you, Tito Joe will benefit from it. Once I get ownership of the farm, only you will be allowed to stay. You can manage it for me. If you decide not to go along with my plan, you can start packing your bags and move your family to the squatter areas of Manila."

Joe is silent, fearful.

"Tito, you're thinking again. I need to know if you are with me on this."

Joe looks at his niece and says bitterly. "I don't see that I have a choice. You are blackmailing me. It's not like you're making me an offer I can back out of!"

He listens to Jenny's hateful schemes. As if hypnotized, he watches her snap her fan open and shut.

"OK. What is the plan?" He is miserable. There is no way out for him.

Jenny smiles. Inside she screams with laughter. She knows that Joe will not benefit from any of this. She will not spare him. He will be the first to go. She has no intention of making good on her promise about forgiving his debt. How clever she is.

"This what we're going to do..." She pulls up a chair and tells him some of her plans, but not all.

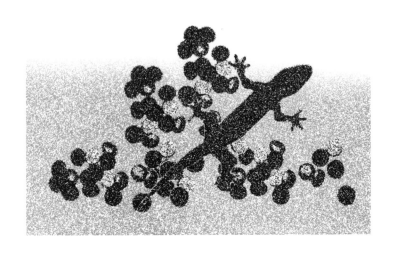

PATRICIA LAUREL

17

More Stories

Up the hill, Lola's family is blissfully unaware of Jenny's plot.

Lola tells them a story she heard as little girl.

"I heard it from an old *yaya* who took care of me and my sister when we were growing up. This is the old *yaya*'s view of the different skin color of people."

"She said that that the Almighty above who created us was teaching himself to bake one day. He was kneading dough and shaped them into human form. He put them all in the oven and forgot a batch sitting nearby. These became the fair skinned people.

"He took some out too early and they came out half baked. These were the brown skinned people. And there were the ones that were over done. They were the dark skinned people. This is the story of how the different races of people began. My sister and I believed it wholeheartedly."

"What about kids like me? Am I a *mestiza*?" Sammy asks.

"Yes, you are a mestiza, which in Spanish means half-half or in Hawai'i you would be a *hapa haole*. This is because you are the product of Jack who is *haole* and Yvonne who is Filipina," Patti explains.

"One more story! Please?" Victoria begs.

"I have one. It's sort of like mommy's story. It's about what kids are led to believe before they learn the truth," Mari says.

Other people join the group. Sammy looks up to see Tito Morris, Tito Larry and Tito Joe, his wife and children. The porch is crowded so they sit on the steps.

After replenishing their drinks, Mari begins her story.

"This is the story of the lizard eggs. When we were just kids, our father pulled a nifty trick on us. Tito Joe, you know this story, you were there."

"Yes, I remember it well. You kids really fell for that one," Joe says, laughing.

All the adults laugh.

"One day some of us were in the living room when Pappy reached up to a shelf on the wall. He brought down his hand in a fist and asked us if we knew what he had. He made us guess, and we all said candy. That was all we could come up with. I mean, what else could it be?

"Pappy said we were close, but not quite. He opened his hand and we saw several little oval shaped things in different colors. He said that they were *butiki* or lizard eggs. My sisters and I reacted with disgust.

"The boys loved to play with them and delighted in torturing us girls by dangling a lizard in front of our faces until its tail fell off. Then they would put the tail on top of one of our heads, still wiggling. Ugh! Icky buggy-eyed creatures! It made us scream!

"Pappy said we should show respect for the *butiki*. They get rid of pesky insects like mosquitoes and gnats. He said that the *butiki* is considered a spritual symbol in other parts of the world. Finally, he said that if we showed the *butiki* a little consideration, we would be rewarded with their delicious eggs. He told us to open our mouths. The girls were reluctant at first, but the boys were eager. We opened our mouths and with eyes tightly shut, Pappy popped them in.

"I let the egg sit on my tongue for a while, afraid of biting into it. Robert was the first to do it. He had that look when someone is eating something really delicious.

"The egg shell began to dissolve in my mouth and I tasted chocolate, so I bit into it. I tasted peanut in the chocolate. Mmm… It was very tasty.

"Pappy had one egg left in his hand. We examined it and saw that there were the letters M&M on it. We asked about the letters. Pappy said that was just so people would know they were *butiki* eggs. We were absolutely thrilled. We promised to treat the *butiki* with respect.

"Robert who always came up with ways to bilk us out of our allowance, suggested that we start searching for the eggs and sell them to our cousins and friends. We would make a bunch of money and divide the profits among ourselves."

Everyone laughs.

"From then on we would search every nook and cranny for the delicious eggs, but never found any unless Pappy was around. He said that we still had a lot to make up for with the *butiki*, but some day we would be rewarded."

"I know what those eggs are!" Victoria says.

"Let mom finish the story," Vernon warns his sister.

"Thank you, Vernon," Mari says.

"We finally discovered the secret of the lizard eggs. Patti went to the store with our cook. She was standing in front of the candy counter looking at all the goodies and noticed yellow packages with the oval eggs and the M&M letters on it. She bought a pack and brought it home to show us. They tasted just like our *butiki* eggs.

"You can imagine our disappointment, especially Robert. But you know what, Pappy's little trick taught us a lesson. The boys stopped torturing the lizards and the girls learned to stop hating them, although sometimes I still shriek when one gets too close."

"That sure was a good story," Tito Joe says, looking at Sammy. "We had a lot of fun with that one."

Sammy has a feeling that Tito Joe is seeing her for the first time. He has an apologetic look. A feeling of apprehension comes to her.

She sees Ollie watching Tito Joe.

Ollie, do you get the feeling that there are people here who know things that can't be good?

Yes. I can sense your uncle knows a secret about you, but he feels bad about it. It's the way he looks at you. We need to find out what's going on.

We have to be careful. Maybe Tito Joe is in trouble. We have to try and help him.

"Oh, look at the time! We need to get going. The people should be arriving for the festivities," Ika says.

"Remember not to stay out too late, and get a good night sleep," Joe says. "We have a very early start tomorrow. It will take us at least a few hours to get to the beach since we're making a couple of stops. Those who want to walk should meet at my house and the others can take the boat."

He pats Sammy on the head and walks down the hill with his wife and kids.

The porch is empty. Everyone has gone down to enjoy the fiesta.

In a few days, their world will be turned upside down.

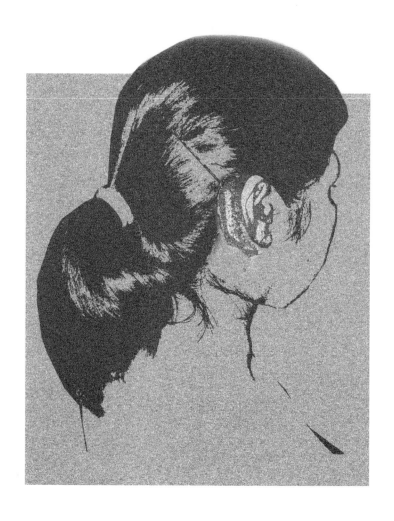

PATRICIA LAUREL

The Fish Girl

Sammy and her cousins can hardly sleep, anticipating the fun day ahead. Air mattresses and sleeping cots occupy most of the floor space of the tents and houses. Most of the family will make the trek to the beach tomorrow.

Sammy wakes to find everyone, even Victoria, up at dawn. People come and go from the three houses, hauling boxes, ice chests, food baskets, drinks and all sorts of picnic gear. The girls watch from the porch as the people wind up and down the hill, like a procession of ants.

Finally everything is ready. The family walk to the train station where Lola and the older aunts and uncles have gathered. They will take the skates to town, and from there board boats to cross the bay.

Yvonne puts on her cap. "Does everyone have a hat? I know it's still cool outside, but soon the sun will be out in full force."

"Let's go! Tito Joe wants us to come on. We have a long walk ahead of us," Larry says.

"Wow! There's a bunch of us walking," Victoria says.

Carabaos stand hitched to carts full of supplies, and a couple of wagons with benches. Joe explains that the wagons are for the really young kids and for those who get tired of walking. He goes back into the house to get his children.

Men wearing straw hats and big leather belts will lead the carabaos. They all carry long knives.

Milly shows up with one of the knives dangling from her waist.

"Those things look wicked," Vernon says.

"This a *bolo* knife. It's very useful when you're walking, especially where there are tall grasses and overgrown bushes. You see how it's curved? It helps cut a path," Milly explains.

Milly starts passing out hand towels. "For later when the sun gets hot," she says. "We'll dip them in cold water and hang them around our necks."

Oh, no! Look who's coming with us! Ollie whispers in Sammy's mind.

Sammy turns to find Jenny standing right behind her, staring.

She's glaring at me, like she wants to put me in an oven and eat me for breakfast, Ollie. Sammy giggles.

Stay away from her, Sammy. Let's go to your mother and your aunts.

Before Jenny can say something, Ollie takes Sammy by the hand and hurries over to where the others are gathered.

Joe puts his children in a wagon, grinning like a kid, but the smile freezes when he sees Jenny. She approaches and says something; he nods curtly and walks away. Sammy has the feeling that Tito Joe's day has been ruined.

She wonders why Jenny is so mean to people.

"Sammy, look!" Ollie says excitedly.

Jenny turns and heads back to her bungalow. Sammy hears a collective sigh of relief.

Joe's grin returns, wider than before. "C'mon, let's go!"

He leads them toward the trail behind his house. Morris is with him. Joe claps his nephew on the shoulder and says, "It's going to be a great day for a picnic!"

The group marches happily along, followed by the men leading the carabaos.

Regal coconut palms line the path like soldiers on guard. "It feels like we've entered a world where the coconut is king," Sammy says to Yvonne.

Yvonne smiles at her daughter and says, "It is true, the coconut rules these parts. You can go on for miles and, all you will see until you get to the beach are the coconut trees. This is how the farm survives. We have mango, banana, jackfruit, rambutan and others, but the coconut harvest every 45 days or so is what keeps this place going."

The fronds of the tall coconut trees clatter with the breeze, but the sun is breaking through and soon will bring its overpowering heat.

Chapter 18 ~ The Fish Girl

They reach the fish hatchery. The carabaos are led into the shade. Cool water is passed around. Sammy takes off with her cousins to explore.

The hatchery has several square pools of salt water. There are a couple of small huts where the people who tend the hatchery live. Mostly shrimp and tilapia are harvested here. The workers share in the harvest, selling their catch at the market in town.

The people say the harvest has not been good lately. "The days are gone when the bay was clean and there was no illegal fishing. There were many fish and shrimp when coral reefs thrived," Joe says with sadness in his voice.

"Tito Joe," Patti says. "We need to start a clean-up project for the bay. People are polluting the bay, not to mention the rivers and creeks. We have got to come up with a plan."

"I'm game. Let's talk about this tomorrow at the family meeting. I've been wanting to do something, but I need the back up, financial that is."

"We'll work something out. I am convinced if we don't do something soon, our way of life here will never be the same."

"How right you are," Joe says. He looks around and his gaze falls on Sammy. It's the same look he had at the story telling on the porch.

Sammy walks over and looks up at him. "Are you OK, Tito Joe?"

"What? Oh, sure. I'm fine. Just remembering back when life was simple and people were real. And look who's here to welcome us with snacks," he says, walking toward the hut.

Nanay Gustia, Eva, Ligaya and Daniel wait for them at the hut with cantaloupe drinks and fresh grilled sweet bananas.

Daniel, Ligaya and Eva serve the refreshments, while Nanay Gustia tends the grill.

After the morning *merienda*, Sammy sits on the floor of the hut, takes out her journal and starts to write down her thoughts. She looks up to see Tito Joe watching her, but he turns away quickly and walks outside. She scribbles in large letters: WHAT IS WRONG WITH TITO JOE? She closes her journal and puts it back in her pack.

She sees Ollie between Daniel and Ligaya on a bench outside. They are asking her more questions about her life in the orphanage. Ollie seems happy to oblige. Eva sits with her grandmother on another bench, listening.

Sammy watches Nanay Gustia's dark leathery face that has seen so many suns and her shy granddaughter, Eva with the slits behind her ears.

Patti joins her niece inside the hut.

"What is the story of Nanay Gustia and Eva, Tita Patti?" Sammy asks.

"All I know is what the locals say. I don't know if there is any truth to it, but it is a good story. Want to hear it?"

Chapter 18 ~ The Fish Girl

"Yes, please!" Sammy says.

"Nanay Gustia has been a healer in these parts for a long time. People say she spends most of her time sitting on a log by the ocean, as if waiting for someone's return. It is whispered that her daughter was enchanted by a creature from the sea. This being transformed itself into a man when he first laid eyes on Nanay Gustia's daughter, Magda. She was beautiful, with long black curly hair and dark eyes. He saw Nanay Gustia combing Magda's long hair one day and was smitten.

"As befitted the custom, the tall, handsome man presented himself to the mother and daughter, and offered to do the manly chores around the house. He said his name was Vicente. He pointed across the bay and said that was where he lived with parents. That was all they knew of him.

"Being a widow, Nanay Gustia gladly accepted his offer. Magda was very pleased because she also felt a great attraction for the mysterious man who suddenly appeared in their lives. Later, Nanay Gustia agreed to their marriage. The couple were very happy and even the neighbors, who were at first suspicious of Vicente, welcomed him.

"A year later, a daughter was born. There was much celebration and feasting for days, and even the man's parents came to the first night of the feast. It was said that the parents were proud, tall and beautiful, but cold like fish. They ignored Nanay Gustia and her daughter. They inspected their granddaughter sleeping in the crib and called for their son. The last time anyone saw Vicente was when he walked with his parents along the beach. They disappeared among the mangrove trees.

"Mother and daughter were abandoned. Magda crossed the bay to where Vicente said he lived with his parents. All she found was a rocky shore with sea gulls perched on the rocks and mangrove trees. Magda was broken hearted. She became listless and spent her days staring out at the ocean. She stopped caring for her daughter Eva. Then one day she just vanished. It was said that she swam out to sea to look for her husband. She was never seen again.

"So Nanay Gustia cared for Eva. She was born with slits behind her ears. People feared her, said that she possessed magical powers. But after a while, they accepted her. Even before Eva could walk, she swam in the ocean. She became the lifeguard of the people who lived on the beach. The parents were at ease when she was around to watch the children swim.

"The slits behind her ears enable her to breathe under water like a fish. She patrols the ocean. Part of her daily routine is to take a plastic bag and a stick with a pointed tip and spend a long time in the water. When she emerges, the bag is full of garbage that she picked off the ocean floor or found floating on the surface."

"Can we help Eva clean the ocean?" Sammy asks her aunt.

"She and I have talked about the dying coral reefs caused by dynamite fishing," Patti says. "People throw explosives into the water and wait for the dead fish to float to the

Chapter 18 ~ The Fish Girl

surface. You cannot imagine the damage it does to the reefs."

Eva walks into the hut. She says something to Patti.

"Eva and I are going to bring up the subject of garbage dumping and illegal fishing tomorrow at the meeting. This cannot go on. Do you want to come to the meeting, Sammy?" Patti asks.

"For sure, Tita Patti," Sammy says. "Ollie and I saw the little creek in town filled with stinking garbage and wished that someone would do something. Maybe people can start recycling here, like we do in California." She looks at Eva, who grins broadly. Finally someone is listening to the fish girl.

"Meantime, I think it's time for us to go to the beach," Patti says, taking Sammy's hand and leading her outside.

19

Fun at the Beach

The group stops along the trail leading to the beach. Daniel and the men leading the carabaos take out their *bolo* knives to clear scrub brush.

"Hey Milly, why don't you help the men clear the path? You've got your bolo knife with you," Yvonne says.

"I don't think I have the strength after my stomach crisis. Besides, I don't want to disturb any cobras lurking about."

"Did I ever tell you about my dance with the cobra?" Joe asks.

Morris laughs. "I thought they only did that in India."

"One day, I was sitting out on the patio," Joe says. "My youngest son was sleeping in a crib when suddenly this cobra appeared. I slowly went over to my son. It started slinking toward me with its hooded head raised. Within striking distance, hissing. If it attacked, it would get me right on the belly and that would be the end of me.

"I started swaying to the left and then to the right, and the cobra did the same. I thought about running. But my little boy would be left unprotected.

"My son was sleeping peacefully on his side. The cobra was ready, its head reared back.

PATRICIA LAUREL

"I jumped on my son's crib. It crashed to the ground, knocking over a table and chair. It was loud enough for my wife to come out and set the dogs barking. My son was squalling. It took a while to untangle myself. The cobra had disappeared.

"That was my dance with the cobra," Joe says to their laughter. "You think it's funny now, but it sure wasn't at the time."

The trail is cleared and the group continues.

"We're here! Look, there's the ocean," Yvonne says, taking Sammy's hand.

They hurry to the clearing, and there to Sammy's delight, is the wide expanse of the sandy beach. The feeling of walking from a lush, jungle scene — and next thing you know — the green landscape turns into miles of sand and blue water that go on forever, is like a dream. It is beautiful.

"Wow, Mom, isn't this great?" Sammy says, dragging Yvonne to the beach.

"I don't know why it took me so long to come back. I don't remember this. I was too young when it happened," Yvonne says in a whisper only Sammy could hear.

"When what happened, mom?"

"Oh, you know. When I left. I sort of remember my father taking me across the bay into town, but the rest is fuzzy.

Let's go to the rest house so you can change into your swimsuit, Sammy."

The rest house is actually Nanay Gustia and Eva's home. The house stands on stilts, a little ways from the beach under some large trees. Lola and the others are already there.

The stilts are wrapped with wire surrounding the area under the house that serves as a chicken coop. A pigpen and vegetable garden are some distance away.

Sammy clutches the handrail as she climbs the steps to the porch. There are a couple of wooden benches with bright pillows. She looks over the railing and sees Eva approach the bottom part of the hut with a pail. Eva bends down and opens the gate to feed the chickens. She comes out a little later with a basket of eggs. Next, she goes to the pen and feeds the pigs snorting happily as they gobble up their food.

The floor of the house is made of bamboo slats and Sammy sees the clucking chickens underneath. The walls are covered with *banig* or woven mats also used for sleeping on the floor. The kitchen is a wooden counter top with a big clay urn for water, a portable gas stove and a sink. A big-screened window overlooks the garden, the outhouse and an enclosed shower stall with no roof.

The house has no bedrooms. Rolled up woven *banig* mats for sleeping are behind a wooden screen in a corner.

PATRICIA LAUREL

Lola sits in a wicker rocking chair in the main room. "I gave this to Gustia as a house warming present when Lolo built this house for her."

"Lola, I could live here. It is so peaceful."

"Would you give up what you have back in San Francisco?"

"Well, there's school, but I could spend my summer vacations here. Don't you think?"

"We'll see what your parents say."

Sammy goes behind the screen, changes into her bathing suit and leaves her grandmother to rest.

The others sit on benches in the dining hut eating watermelon.

"C'mon, let's get in the water," Vernon says, tugging at Victoria. He wears goggles, ready to explore.

They run happily to the water, joining the other cousins frolicking and splashing each other. Sammy takes out her journal, ever mindful of Solo's advice.

"Tito Marc, where do Daniel and Ligaya live?" she asks.

"I'm not sure," her uncle says, spitting out a watermelon seed.

"If you head that way, along the bay," he points with his spoon, "you come to a bend where there is a lagoon with a lot of mangrove trees. Further in, it turns into a marsh. That is where we get the water for the fish hatchery.

"Anyway, their home lies hidden among the mangrove trees and you better know where you're going and how to navigate a boat. It is easy to lose your way. People say it can get really spooky. And you never know when an *engkanto* might decide to play with you."

Sammy seizes her pen excitedly, "Can you tell me the meaning of *engkanto* again, Tito Marc?"

Marc laughs. "What a little journalist you are, writing everything down. An *engkanto* is an enchanted creature. Daniel," he calls, "come tell Sammy about your adventure with the *tikbalang*."

Daniel comes and sits with them.

"You remember the big Banyan tree by Morris's pig pens, back behind Milly's house?" Marc says.

Sammy nods, writing.

"Here we call it a *balete* tree. Daniel always warned me that if I ever go near one, I must ask permission to pass from whoever dwells there. But he forgot to do it himself one time. Tell her about the spell that was cast on you, Daniel."

"Do you really want me to?" Daniel says, his eyes widening. "It may scare the child."

Marc waves his spoon dismissively. "Tell her. She wants to know all the stories from around here."

"Very well, Kuya Marc." Before he starts his story, Daniel strikes a match. "For protection," he says.

Despite her eager curiosity, Sammy feels a chill creep up the back of her neck. She fingers the *anting-anting* Ollie made for her.

A few years ago Daniel had been fishing in a creek on the farm. A place where he knows the layout of the land like the back of his hand.

One day after a particularly good catch, he headed down the trail and passed by Morris's pig farm. He noticed the *balete* tree at the edge of the trail, but forgot to ask permission to cross its path.

It became clear that he was going the wrong way when he ended up right back at the tree. This happened several times and it was getting dark. He had to throw his catch away because the fish had gone bad. He looked up at the tree and saw that the leaves were rustling, as if it were being shaken. But the air was as still as the grave, and no birds could be heard.

He realized he had forgotten to pay his respects to the one who ruled the space around the tree. He had offended the *tikbalang*. The elders say that the creature is half man and half horse and any encounter with it should be avoided.

He tried every trick he could think of to appease the creature that was tormenting him. Daniel lit matches, walked backward and even took his clothes off and wore them inside out. The last resort was to show his behind and even that didn't work.

"I was in despair," Daniel says. "I had a deep fear in my belly," he pauses to rub his stomach, "that I would never get home to Ligaya, that I would wander forever, lost in the forest.

"Finally," he says, "I got down on my knees and prayed like never before. I got up, trembling, and tried the trail one more time. I walked with my head down, afraid to look up, because I knew that once again, I would find myself in front of the tree. I walked forever.

"But, *Salamat sa Diyos* —Thank the Lord — a miracle happened."

He found himself miles away, standing at his house on the lagoon with the mangrove trees, and his wife demanding to know where he had been. With tears of joy, he hugged her fiercely and swore never to disrespect any creature of the land.

"Wow!" Sammy says giggling. "You even showed your behind."

"A friend told me he did that one time and it worked," Daniel says, smiling sheepishly.

"Did you see the *tikbalang*, Daniel?" Sammy asks.

"Not really, but I heard the clicking sound it makes and that was scary," Daniel says. He gives a little bow because his story is finished and rejoins the other men by the carabaos.

"Tito Marc, do you believe in all that stuff?"

PATRICIA LAUREL

"I'm not superstitious, but there was that one time. I was walking from Milly's house to the station in the dark to take the skate back to town. Someone tapped me on the shoulder. I turned around, there was no one there. It happened several times. You know what I did?"

Sammy shakes her head.

"I beat feet and ran like crazy to Ika's house. I spent the night there and didn't go to town until the next morning."

"Did you show your behind like Daniel?" Sammy asks, as Robert walks up.

"Sure he did," Robert says. "I've done it plenty of times myself. Oh yeah, the shoulder tapping happened to me many times."

Sammy catches him winking at his brother. "You're making it up!" she says.

Robert laughs, then turns serious.

"Around here, when it's pitch black outside it's best to stay indoors. People say the humans have the daytime and the night creatures get their turn after dark. That's how we live peacefully with the *engkantos*."

"What about if you have a flashlight or you're with a bunch of people?" Sammy asks.

"That's different. If you're with a group, the thing won't show itself. Once it's known that an *engkanto* is inhabiting the area, Nanay Gustia will be called on to ask it to go away."

Sammy sees Eva approach Yvonne and Milly with several plastic bags and long, pointed sticks.

"It's time for us to go pick up trash," Milly says, taking a plastic bag and a stick from Eva.

Sammy looks at her cousins splashing and yelling in the water and then at the plastic bags.

Yvonne bails her out. "Sweetie, go and join your cousins. There will be enough opportunity for you to help us with the clean-up project. Go on, have fun!"

20

Ollie's Trip

Ollie, where are you going?

Don't worry, Sammy. Daniel and Ligaya asked me if I wanted to see their house. Mama Ika said it would be OK.

Do you want me to come with you?

I'll be fine. You look like you're having fun swimming with your cousins. I'll see you later.

OK. Bye.

Ollie sits in the prow of the motorboat, which skims the blue-green water of the cove. She is daydreaming, gazing out at the far horizon where the water of the South China Sea melts into the blue sky. Everything happens so fast. A few days ago she was an orphan, now Mama Ika and the whole clan have taken her in.

Not to mention meeting Sammy, the best friend she has ever had. It makes her head spin.

Daniel sits in the stern by the outboard motor, which is very noisy and smoky. Ligaya, who sits between them, smiles and holds her hands over her ears. The motor makes such a racket they shout to be heard.

"Not far now!" Daniel yells and points ahead.

PATRICIA LAUREL

Ollie sees a green wall of mangrove trees. She knows it is the entrance to a wide, shallow lagoon, and deep inside it they will come to Daniel and Ligaya's thatched home on the edge of a narrow white beach.

A school of fish begins to leap out of the water, flashing in the sunshine.

A wave of happiness wells up inside the little girl and she realizes she dreamt this scene many times before. She knows what will happen now.

Everything is falling into place for Ollie.

Daniel cuts the motor back as they enter the lagoon. The passage through the twisted mangrove trees is so narrow that anyone watching from a distance would think the boat and its three occupants have vanished into the green maze. They emerge onto the bright blue lagoon, which is the most beautiful, tranquil place Ollie has ever seen. The water is crystal clear, and looking over the side, Ollie sees the sandy bottom. Everywhere there are schools of fish brimming through the water, crabs, shellfish. Gulls and cranes flutter up in white clouds at the noise of the motor.

Ollie sees the little thatched house on stilts on the gleaming white beach. There are coconut palms and a garden of flowers and vegetables.

She knows what her room will look like, with its comfy little bed and the clothes her size that hang in the closet. She belongs here. She is meant to sit on that porch and look out over this lovely, quiet lagoon with Daniel and Ligaya sitting near her.

Ollie hears Ligaya's voice.

Daniel, we have to tell her now. I can't wait any longer; my heart is about to burst.

All right, Ligaya, we tell her now.

The motor is still so loud, how can she hear them? Suddenly Ollie knows. Mind talk. She, Ligaya and Daniel are all looking at each other — smiling.

Daniel cuts the motor off and they glide up to the beach.

Mixed Feelings...

Joe sits on the bench with his nephews watching the delighted children squeal and splash. His sister-in-law Marita and her daughter Ika chat on Gustia's porch, while his other nieces help Eva the fish girl clean up the beach.

He looks at his nephews whom he considers his own since their father passed away. Maybe he could tell them his problem. Pride and shame stop him. He winces at the thought of asking for help, but also because the old pain in his leg has flared up.

"Tito Joe, you hurting?" Morris asks.

"It's just the souvenir of my guerrilla days," Joe says, rubbing the long purple scar on his leg.

Joe still has bad dreams about the Death March and fighting in the war. The Japanese soldier squinting down the barrel of the carbine as he and his brother Bobby stumble and run through the jungle, crazy from thirst. The bullets thud into the tree trunks and then the blazing pain in his leg.

Bobby drags him underneath some bushes and hides behind a tree. Joe remembers that Bobby was crouched down holding a big rock. "He was going to fight against rifles and machine guns with a rock," Joe often says.

PATRICIA LAUREL

"Bobby would have fought a tiger with a toothpick, if he had to."

They escaped that day. Finally wandered upon a village of fishermen who dressed his wound, put the two brothers in a dugout canoe and took them to the guerrilla camp.

They became scouts for the Americans, he and his brother Bobby did.

Joe's favorite story from the war days isn't about heroism or gallant battles. It is a funny story. He has told it many times.

"We were scouts, leading the Americans up to a Japanese camp in Laguna," he would say. "The troops formed a crescent line, like a half-moon shape. Bobby was at one end of the line and I was at the other, the two points.

"Creeping up on the Japanese camp across the river. We could hear them talking, their voices carrying across the water in the night. We could smell the food they were cooking."

His nieces and nephews would always draw closer when he told that part, he and Bobby so close to the Japanese soldiers that they could breath on them.

"When the time was right, we opened fire and they ran. Completely surprised, they panicked. When we went into the camp, we found a brand new Studebaker truck. Brand new. It looked so beautiful. Bobby and I liberated it. We

Chapter 21 ~ Mixed Feelings...

used that truck for years after the war was finally over, when we got the farm going again."

When Yvonne was a little girl, someone had asked her what her daddy did in the war. Right away she piped up, "My Pappy and Tito Joe stole a beautiful Studebaker from the Japanese."

People always laughed at that.

Joe rubs his leg. You never know how things turn out. Life looked so bleak and hopeless in the war, yet the family survived. Maybe somehow this business with Jenny would work out for the best.

"I think I'll go over to Gustia and have her give me something for my leg. Her homemade medicines always help me," Joe says, getting up.

Soon it is time to eat lunch. Everyone gathers at the dining hut where banana leaves are spread out on the table.

Sammy sees there are no plates. Large platters of food are on the table. She watches as the food is dished up and flopped down in front of her. First comes the rice, and then pork and chicken adobo. There is also *pancit* or rice noodle, steamed shrimp from the hatchery and grilled fish. There are ripe mangoes, whole coconuts with the juice still inside and watermelon.

"Sammy, remember I told you we would be eating with our hands today? This is it. Dig in!" Milly says.

"This is great! We're going to slop down like pigs!" Vernon says with delight. Even Lola who preaches strict manners enjoys eating with her hands.

Sammy soon gets the hang of it. She is digging into her meal with both hands when she feels a tap on her shoulder. Ollie has returned with Daniel and Ligaya. She looks happy, but there is a change in her.

Sammy gestures for her to sit down. Ollie hardly picks at the tempting food.

Did you see Daniel and Ligaya's home?

I love their house. It is so peaceful there. Sammy, they know all about me. They even have a bedroom for me. There are clothes my size in the closet. They want me to live with them.

Sammy's mind is buzzing now.

How could they know all about you? Can they mind talk? How can you live with them if you are adopted by Tita Ika? You''ll go to Germany with her, won't you? What's wrong? Did something happen? There's something you're not telling me. What's going on, Ollie?

Ollie takes a bite of the food and then gives Sammy a helpless look.

Sammy, they are my parents.

Ollie tells Sammy that Daniel and Ligaya took her to the children's home in Manila when she was a baby because

Chapter 21 ~ Mixed Feelings...

they were afraid an enchanted creature of the forest was going to steal her.

They are the ones who were in my dreams, Sammy. They can mind talk like us. They helped put the dreams in Mama Ika's head to take me from the orphanage and bring me here.

Ollie, things are getting too crazy. Do my Lola and Nanay Gustia know?

I think so.

Who is this enchanted forest creature? Is it still around?

I think Nanay Gustia can keep it away. Sammy, I can't tell you everything now. Please give me some time and I will tell you everything soon.

OK, Ollie, OK. But tell me soon, promise. I'm scared.

I promise, Sammy. I will always be your friend.

As Ollie walks over to where Daniel and Ligaya help with the food, Sammy thinks about Lolo Ciano, wishing that he would show up. He would know what to do.

The table is cleared after lunch and the grownups sit around talking. Patti and the kids stroll back to the water. Eva is with them carrying a plastic bag and sharp stick. Sammy and her cousins watch as the fish girl dives underwater and is gone for a long time.

"Where did she go? She's going to drown!" Victoria says, getting up and looking out on the horizon.

"Wow! Look, there she is." Vernon shouts.

Eva surfaces in the distance. Her head looks like a black dot bopping up and down as she swims back to them. Her plastic bag is full.

"She's not even breathing hard," Vernon says in awe.

The cousins look inside the plastic bag. It is full of old plastic bottles, soda cans and other things that do not belong at the bottom of the sea.

"She's been picking trash from the ocean," Sammy says. "My dad says that if we don't pay attention, all living things in the ocean will die because of all the garbage that is dumped into it."

"When we were kids, you could stroll on the beach and see all kinds of beautiful sea shells. Now dead coral and broken sea shells litter the beach along with a lot of garbage," Patti says angrily.

They pick up trash all afternoon. Many bags are collected and placed in the carts hitched to the carabaos that are heading back to the compound.

All too soon the picnic ends. The sun starts its slow descent. The family climb into the boats that will take them to town, from there they will ride the skates to the farm.

Sammy takes out her journal, crosses out the question marks by Daniel and Ligaya's names, and replaces them with check marks.

Chapter 21 ~ Mixed Feelings...

Now she knows who all her guides are.

Meanwhile...

In Manila, a man in white sits on a bench in Luneta Park. People pass without seeing him. He watches the changing of the guard at his brother's monument.

I am so proud of you, Pepe. It was a good thing you did. For my part, I am sad that you were taken during your prime, but I do not regret sending you away to further your education. You made the world aware of the injustice and suffering of the Filipino people. But I'm afraid this time our people are suffering at the hands of their own kind.

Lola Ciano looks around him. He is not happy with what he sees. There are so many poor people and children living in hovels, under bridges and in abandoned vehicles. Back in the 1950s and well into the 1960s, things were progressing in the right direction and the people were united.

In the late 1960s, everything changed. A vicious, greedy man became president. His long misrule brought the country to its knees. The treasury was looted. He imposed martial law and imprisoned his enemies, sometimes taking their lives.

The way of life Lolo Ciano envisioned for his people has deteriorated, maybe to the point of no return. Only the rich have gotten richer and are too selfish to share.

He feels a presence next to him.

"Pepe!"

The brothers hug.

"You're seeing misery, Kuya Ciano. It is a sad thing when you see countless homeless people sleeping in the park, teaching their children to beg and steal. I see very desperate people.

"Do you remember the beautiful Manila Bay sunsets? What do you see now? A brown shroud smothers the sun's orange and pink rays."

"Come, Pepe. Let's go for a walk."

If people could see these two men dressed in old-fashioned attire, they would surely wonder. The shorter man in the suit and the taller man in *barong Tagalog*. The two men from history talking of what should be done to alleviate the suffering of their people.

[196]
PATRICIA LAUREL

The Ball of Light

They eat a light supper in town before heading back. Skates wait at the train station. The group is happy and loud when they start out. But they fall quiet when the twinkling lights from the town disappear. Only a few feeble flashlights from the skates pierce the inky night.

Sammy concentrates on sounds. While the skates sputter along the tracks, she hears the constant chirping of crickets and the eerie rustle of flapping wings.

People around her are silent, peering into the darkness.

Yvonne grips Jack's arm fearfully.

"Mom, what's wrong?" Sammy asks.

"Oh, she's afraid something will jump out from the dark and whisk her off," Jack says, laughing. Then he sees tears trickling down his wife's face.

"Hey, I was just kidding," he says, putting his arms around her.

"Here, mom. Hold on to my *anting-anting*," Sammy places the charm bracelet Ollie gave her in her mother's hands.

As soon as her mother touches the charm, the fear on her face turns to an embarrassed smile. "Thank you Sammy. I don't know what happened. I felt the night closing in on me and I couldn't breathe."

"Look! Look up ahead!" Jack says suddenly.

A huge flickering ball of light hangs in the sky. Sammy thinks of a big Christmas ornament.

The skates slow down. To one side is a big tree covered with bright lights that hop about its branches.

"I have never seen so many fireflies in all my years," Joe says.

"There must be thousands of them in that tree," Mari says.

"This is waaaay cool," Vernon says.

"Our driver says that there are good spirits at work here. They are showing us our way home," Patti says.

They get off the skates and stand looking at the tree.

"They look like tiny shooting stars," Victoria says.

"I've seen those lights before," Morris says.

"Really? Were you lost in the dark, Tito Morris?" Vernon asks.

"You could say that," Morris says, looking at Yvonne.

When they arrive safely at the little station, Yvonne still seems embarrassed, but calmer.

"Are you all right, Mom? Sammy asks. "You looked so spooked."

"I'm OK. I guess I'm not used to it being so dark. I just don't remember what it's like out here on the farm." Yvonne says, frowning as if trying to remember something.

Yvonne exchanges hurried whispers with her brothers and sisters.

"Jack, can you manage the kids for a bit?" Yvonne asks.

Jack raises an eyebrow, but nods his head.

The aunts and uncles follow Yvonne to Milly's house.

Sammy watches her mother walk up the hill with her brothers and sisters. She wishes she could be there to listen. Secrets will be revealed tonight.

[200]
Patricia Laurel

Morris's Story...

Up at Milly's house, Yvonne finally asks the question that has been gnawing at her. "Do any of you remember anything that happened when I was about 3 years old? It happened here. I remember a boat ride with Pappy holding me in his arms."

"Milly and I were at school in Madrid," Ika says, shaking her head.

"I was too young," Marc says.

"What I remember is our summer vacation here was cut short. We were taken back to San Pablo in a hurry," Mike says.

Robert, Patti and Mari nod in agreement.

"All I remember is that I was waiting in town for Morris with Tito Joe. We drove away from there as if we were being chased by the devil himself. I tried to ask Pappy later, but he wouldn't tell me," Larry says, looking at Morris.

Morris stands by the window, looking out at the night. He turns around. "Yvonne, what do you remember?"

"My memory is very patchy, but tonight something about the dark really frightened me. I seem to remember being surrounded by thousands of flickering light in the forest. Was it the fireflies?"

Morris nods, studying his youngest sister.

"Our first day here," Yvonne says. "Sammy stood by the mango tree like she was hypnotized. I steered her quickly away from it. When I was small, I stood by that tree. I was crying until someone picked me up."

Morris looks like someone has struck him. "NO! You need to stay away from that tree, especially Sammy. Do you understand?"

They all look at him.

"What is going on? Morris, please tell me," Yvonne pleads.

Morris sits down. Of all the brothers, he is the one who most resembles their father. "When Yvonne was 3 years old," he says, "she was almost snatched by that thing that lives in the mound beside the mango tree."

"What are you saying? What thing?" Ika asks.

Morris looks at the floor. Their mother and Nanay Gustia enter the house.

"Morris, go on," their mother says, "tell it."

"We never told any of you what happened," Morris says. "Mommy and Pappy said that it would be best to keep it quiet.

"We were all here for the summer, except for mommy who stayed in San Pablo to prepare for our departure. We knew that we were leaving for the U.S. and were excited, but sad

PATRICIA LAUREL

at the same time because Pappy would not be traveling with us."

"But what about the mango tree?" Yvonne asks.

"There was nothing on this hill, except overgrown grass, bamboo everywhere and that mango tree," Morris says. "There was a path from our old house that led to it and then went on to the creek."

"It happened when Ligaya and Gustia were watching Yvonne," Lola says. "Ligaya was just a girl. Gustia was working in the house and asked Ligaya to watch Yvonne."

Morris looks at Yvonne again, then continues the story.

"Daniel, Ligaya's sweetheart, showed up and she became focused on him. It was a little while later when they noticed that Yvonne was no longer there. They thought she was playing hide and seek. But she had vanished. Their shouts brought Nanay Gustia out of the house. They searched everywhere, but they couldn't find her.

"I have never seen Pappy afraid except that one time. He had us frantically searching everywhere. Suddenly, Nanay Gustia started running down the path that led to mango tree. We followed, running.

"There was Yvonne. She was standing near the tree, but it was the mound beside it that held her attention. There was no wind, but a swirl of dust mixed with grass and leaves was whipping around on top of the mound. You were crying, sis, but your hand was reaching out for the swirl."

Chapter 23 ~ Morris's Story...

Yvonne nods, tears running down her face.

"That was when we saw him," Morris says. "I had never believed in the *duwende*, but there he was beckoning to Yvonne. It seemed like everything was in slow motion. And then I heard Nanay Gustia chanting beside me clasping the *anting-anting*, the charm, she wore around her neck."

Nanay Gustia stands in the door with her eyes shut, clutching the charms around her neck, living the memory. "Oh, how I chanted that day," she says. "I chanted and prayed with all my might."

"She broke the spell," Morris says. "Daniel snatched up Yvonne as the swirl was about to pull her in. Nanay Gustia quickly placed a charm on Yvonne's neck, and Pappy took her from Daniel.

"I turned around to see the *duwende* stomping the ground, full of rage. He pointed a sword at the dusty swirl and it lurched at us like a little tornado.

"We ran like crazy back to the house. Pappy slammed the door. We looked out the window to see the swirling wind swaying and sucking in toys and flowerpots. The *duwende* appeared beside it and pointed at the house.

"The *duwende* shouted that Yvonne had trespassed on his domain. It is the rule of the earth creatures and humans must abide by it! If Pappy did not give him Yvonne, he would track her down. Believe me when I tell you this, the *duwende* said, I will take her.

"Pappy walked outside. I thought he was going to fight, but his words were calm.

"Pappy told the *duwende*, this land has been in my family for generations. Your domain sits on our land. Now we know you exist. Did you ever inform us humans about this rule? You have no right to any claims on people under my protection.

"The *duwende* was furious. He said he had been here since the Spanish arrived. He needed permission from no one, he said.

"Pappy didn't flinch. He said, that may be true, *duwende*, but I can call on healers to come and purge your kind from my farm. Do you want me to do that?

"They dickered and bargained, bluffed and threatened. The *duwende* said if Pappy promised not to take Yvonne away from the farm until she became an adult, he would compromise. Yvonne would spend the days with the *duwende* and go home to her family at sunset. The *duwende* would have her during the day to keep him company and he promised to send her home before dark.

"Pappy gave him a hard look and said, what do you take me for, *duwende*?

"The *duwende* made sweet promises. He would treat Yvonne like his own. He only wanted her as a companion during the daytime. He promised riches for our family. I am from the earth and I know where precious gems can be found, he said rubbing his hands.

"Yvonne is my precious gem, Pappy said. No cold stone would ever replace her."

Yvonne sobs, wiping more tears from her face.

"Finally, Pappy said that he would think about it and let the *duwende* know in a couple of days," Morris continues. "I knew Pappy was playing for time.

"The *duwende* warned him, don't let me wait too long. Then he vanished.

"Pappy sent the other kids back to San Pablo. He told Larry to go to town and wait there with Tito Joe.

"Pappy and I rode the horses to the beach where Nanay Gustia lived. He carried you wrapped in a blanket, Yvonne. And then something really incredible happened. We would have become lost with only a lantern to guide us, if not for the fireflies. They appeared out of nowhere and soon there were thousands of little lights streaking through the trail.

"Nanay Gustia, Daniel and Ligaya were waiting for us. Pappy and Yvonne got into the boat with Daniel and Ligaya. I stayed behind with Nanay Gustia. We would leave for San Pablo almost immediately.

"We saw a flash of red and orange light up the sky and heard an explosion. I'm sure Pappy saw it from the boat.

"The *duwende* had destroyed our home, burned it with a fireball. Nanay Gustia brought out a bag of iron spikes from her house, and we rode the horses back.

"When we got to the farm the house was just a pile of smoking ashes," Morris says. "People said they saw sparks flying from the mango tree to our house before it exploded.

"Nanay Gustia gathered the people and had us form a circle around the mound and the mango tree. She started to chant while the *duwende* was still weak from all the magic he created. She drove the spikes into the earth, making a circle around the mound."

Lola says, "Gustia warned the people never to remove the spikes. She performed a magic spell to keep the *dwende* from capturing another child."

"We left for the U.S. the next day," Morris says. "I talked with Pappy on the phone about a month later and he said that the mound was smaller, more like a small anthill. Nanay Gustia's charms worked."

"Nanay Gustia checked again today," Lola says. "The spikes are still there, in the tall grass around the mound. But she doesn't think you should stay here now. She has a sense that something bad is brewing. I agree with her. She says the *duwende* has been seen walking around. His magic will be more powerful if the spikes are removed."

Yvonne wipes her tears. "I want to leave this place," she says.

They decide to return to San Pablo immediately after the fiesta.

"Don't tell the children," Lola says. "There is no use in frightening them. But keep them away from that mango tree."

Chapter 23 ~ Morris's Story...

Outside, in a dark corner of Milly's porch someone sits on a bench and listens.

"Of course!" Joe whispers.

Stumbling in the Dark

Sammy anxiously waits for her mother's return. Music blares in the courtyard filled with people, ready for another night of fun and feasting.

She feels uneasy.

She sees her mother walking beside Lola. Her aunts and uncles follow with Nanay Gustia. She runs to her mother.

"The fiesta has started. Are we going now?" Sammy asks.

Yvonne hugs her daughter. "Yes, dear. We are all going. Go get your dad. I need to talk to him before we go. Hold my hand, Sammy. I want you close to me tonight."

When the big stars come out, the fiesta comes to life with merry music, colored lanterns bobbing in the night and happy shouts and laughter. But somehow the mood has been dampened. Sammy can sense the adults' pretense at having fun.

Up on the hill by the mango tree, two figures in the moonlight are grimly searching in the tall grass with a dim flashlight.

"Are you sure you heard her right? The spikes are here somewhere? Why do you move so slowly?"

"My leg is bothering me. My war wound. Be patient."

PATRICIA LAUREL

"Your leg, your war wound, it's always something with you, Tito Joe."

Jenny falls hard on the ground.

"OW! Something tripped me. I think I turned my ankle."

"Not so loud, Jenny."

Joe shines the flashlight where she stumbled.

"Wait, there's an iron spike, just like Gustia said. Get up, we must find them all."

"Of course," Jenny grumbles. "It took me to find the first one. Help me up."

Meanwhile…

In Hawai'i, on the island of O'ahu, in the town of Kailua, Solo paces the sandy beach. His bright eyes search the water for his *aumakua*, his ancestral spirit, the tiger shark.

A fin and a mouth full of sharp teeth emerge from the frothy surf. Solo approaches and whispers. "Help her. I feel something bad is about to happen…"

The sleek, dark form of the tiger shark slices through the waves.

Solo sighs. "I hope it's not too late…"

In Metro Manila, the spirits of brothers Ciano and Pepe visit Fort Santiago in the walled city of Intramuros where Pepe spent his last mortal hours on earth.

The brothers have been in the museum looking at their family tree displayed prominently among the exhibits.

"Look here," Ciano says, pointing to their sister Maria's branch. "These are the descendants of our sister Maria, and this is the little girl I told you about."

They talk of the old days.

"Kuya, do you remember when…?" Pepe asks his older brother. Ciano nods his head and the shared memories tumble out.

All too soon their visit must end.

Pepe turns to his brother. "I think it is time for us to part ways again. Our little girl, Samantha needs you now."

"She is a brave girl, just like the women in the family. Maria's female descendants are especially stubborn and strong willed. Didn't I always say that our sister should have been a man?"

The brothers laugh.

They say their goodbyes. Pepe returns to Luneta Park, and Paciano heads for the province of Quezon.

The Bait

Sammy wakes up just as the sun's rays bring a golden tint to the sky. All is still. The rest of the family is deep in sleep, worn out from last night's festivities.

After the fiesta, the party continued at Milly's house with the older cousins playing music and jamming with their aunts. Even the younger ones, who like rap and hip hop, enjoyed dancing and singing the old tunes.

Later, Sammy and Victoria settles down on the air mattress they share on the living room floor. Yakking and giggling go on until the last whisper, Victoria's of course.

Sammy nimbly steps over her sleeping cousin. She gets her journal, and goes out to the porch.

The crowing of roosters replaces the night sounds of the frogs and crickets. She enjoys waking up to a rooster chorus, better than her tick-tocking Mickey Mouse clock in San Francisco.

The dogs eagerly wag their tails at the sight of the first person to come out of the house. She listens to the happy chirping of birds from the trees and watches the *butiki* skitter away searching for breakfast bugs.

Ika's dog Prieto follows Sammy down the porch steps onto the grass glistening with morning dew. Some of

[214]
PATRICIA LAUREL

the puppies want to follow, but Prieto growls and the whimpering puppies stay put.

Sammy throws her arms out wide and yawns. Now would be a good time to write down her thoughts. She sits on the porch step, opens her journal and begins to write. Her eyes wander to Prieto sniffing the ground. He finds something, licks it up and Sammy hears a tiny crunching sound.

She looks to see what the dog is eating. There on the ground are the colorful lizard eggs. If my cousins were awake, they'd have a feast before breakfast, Sammy chuckles to herself.

She looks to see if anyone is about, maybe one of the uncles pulling a trick.

Sammy pops one of the eggs into her mouth. "Sure does taste like M&M's to me," she says out loud, just in case someone is listening.

The girl in pink pajamas and the big, black dog go happily along the candy trail, past the tents where other family members sleep. Not a soul stirs.

"Zee Land," Sammy whispers to Prieto.

Suddenly Prieto growls. His tail is tucked between his legs. He crawls over to Sammy, whimpering, as if seeking protection.

"It's OK, Prieto. There's no one here," she pats the dog's head.

Chapter 25 ~ The Bait

She does not realize how far she has wandered. She is almost at Milly's house. Before her is the mango tree.

A voice inside her warns of immediate danger. Before Sammy can stop herself, she stumbles on the mound of earth and scatters the dirt.

Sammy recalls Nanay Gustia's warning about disturbing the home of an earth creature.

She quickly pats the dirt back as best she can. She waits a few minutes, breathes a sigh of relief and starts back to the house with Prieto.

The dawn sky darkens. The roosters and birds fall silent. Prieto freezes with one paw in the air. Two puppies frolic on Milly's porch. One on its back and the other about to spring on its playmate. They are statues, just like Prieto beside her.

"I've been waiting a long time for you," a voice says.

Sammy turns around, puzzled. There is no one there. She feels tugging at her pajama pants. She looks down.

Oh no! She instinctively touches her wrist, feeling for the *anting-anting* bracelet Ollie gave her. She forgot to put it back on after washing her hands earlier.

A little brown man whose head is only up to her knees is standing there. He wears an odd hat that looks like a basket and a purple cloth wrapped around his waist. His white beard trails to the ground and he has a little sword in one hand.

She wants a better look at the little man, with his pot belly, knobby knees and elbows, and long, scrawny fingers. Exactly the way he appeared in her dream.

"Who are you and why have you been waiting a long time for me?" Sammy asks. She stares at the gleaming eyes surrounded with dark circles.

"I am the *duwende*. I have a score to settle with your mother, child. You will pay for it and so will the rest of your meddling family."

"What do you mean? What did my mother do to you?"

"Plenty of time to tell you stories when we are underground. We will have all your life to talk," the *duwende* says, his eyes darting around.

"No. My mother would never do anything to you. It isn't true."

"You take after your Lolo. Cunning, deceitful and stubborn."

"My Lolo was a good and brave man."

The *duwende* glares at her. "He cheated me of what was rightly mine!"

Sammy is afraid, but she must keep him talking. "What about my mother?"

The *duwende* smiles.

"Her *yaya* was Gustia, that meddlesome hag. She was careless and left your mother in the care of a lovesick girl.

That was Ligaya. The stupid girl only had eyes for her Daniel. So while they were flirting, Yvonne wandered off. She stepped on my home." He points his sword at Sammy. "Just like you."

"But I didn't mean to." Sammy looks around desperately for someone, anyone.

"ENOUGH! You think I don't see what you're doing? There is no one to protect you now."

The *duwende* can smell the fear on her.

"Come now, it is time for us to leave," he says soothingly, crooking a twisted finger at her.

As the *duwende* is about to conjure up his swirling cloud to suck Sammy in, a white light appears.

"Lolo Ciano!" Sammy cries.

The *duwende*'s face shows shock, then livid anger. He jumps up and down, waving his sword furiously.

"Who are you and what business do you have here?" The *duwende* glares at the man in white. "This girl trespassed on my property and she must pay. That is the rule."

"Not my rule, *duwende*," Lolo Ciano says.

"What is this? Another family member to the rescue? You're not even human, you're just a spirit of your former self," the *duwende* says sarcastically.

"*Duwende*, do you know who I am?" Lolo Ciano says. "You came here with the Spanish and their swords and ships. You know the bloodline of this child. You knew that when you tried to take her mother away. What made you think you could do that?"

"I need satisfaction for what has been done to me," the *duwende* says in frustration.

Lolo Ciano, can he really take me with him? Sammy asks in mind talk.

It will be all right, Samantha. Just be ready when you hear me say NOW! Slowly inch your way toward me if you can.

"Don't think I'm stupid," the *duwende* says. "I know about mind talk."

NOW! Lolo Ciano's voice booms in her head. *Don't let him touch you!*

Sammy lunges for her uncle. Too late. The *duwende* jumps up and puts a finger to her lips. Against her will, she feels herself bending down so that she is now eye level with the *duwende*. Her lips are stuck on the *dwende*'s finger! She cannot move. The *duwende*'s hand is cold as ice and freezes her in place.

Lolo Ciano grabs Sammy's wrist and with his other hand yanks the *duwende*'s beard.

The *duwende* releases Sammy with a loud yelp. Sammy looks at Lolo Ciano in astonishment.

Chapter 25 ~ The Bait

Lolo Ciano! How did you do that? You're a spirit, but I felt your hand.

When the spirit is willing, all is possible. But I'm afraid he still managed to work his magic on you.

The *duwende* strokes his beard and looks at them with a grudging respect.

"You will face consequences, little girl," he says to Sammy.

"What are your terms, *duwende*? Talk to me. I am her guardian," Lolo Ciano says.

"You are not allowed to tell anyone what happened, especially that hag Gustia. If you do, I will turn on your cousins. Children will start disappearing around here."

"Agreed. What else?"

"The punishment for Sammy will not be imprisonment underground, but something that will torment her mother, Yvonne." The *duwende* smiles, his dark eyes sly, malicious.

Sammy feels tears welling up, but holds them back. She will not let the *duwende* see her cry.

"When you leave these parts, the instant your feet leave the ground, you will have no voice. You will not be able to talk to anyone; you will not be able to write anything down. Your writing will turn to chicken scratch. No one will understand your messages. Your only communication will be with your spirit uncle here and a lot good that will do," the *duwende* says, with a smirk.

"There is an end to every problem," Lolo Ciano says. "Earth creatures like yourself will give us a great task to perform, and if we succeed, your spell will be broken, am I right?"

"Clever spirit. Yes, that's the condition. I am going to change homes as soon as we're done here. Your task is to find me. I can be a thousand miles from here or anywhere, like a jewel in the earth. If you find me, the girl gets her voice back. And maybe something else too," the *duwende* says.

"Please, *duwende*, give us a clue?" Sammy says desperately.

"No. Enjoy your last few days here. Talk as much as you want, but not about our deal. You will have no choice but to return here. If you're lucky, we may cross paths again. That's all I will tell you," the *duwende* says. He is about to leave, then turns back to Sammy and Lolo Ciano.

"I will say this. There is something else brewing here that you are not aware of. It has nothing to do with our agreement, but a lot to do with some members of your family," the *duwende* says.

After all, Jenny does not please him. Why not make more trouble for the greedy shrew?

"Remember, ONLY IF YOU CAN FIND ME," the *duwende* says gleefully, laughing and rubbing his hands as he walks back to his mound. He is gone in a flash, but Sammy can still hear his echoing laugh.

Chapter 25 ~ The Bait

"Let's leave here quickly," Lolo Ciano says.

Prieto shakes himself and wags his tail when he sees Sammy. The puppies on Milly's porch resume their play. People stir in the tents.

She is almost at the house when Nanay Gustia approaches with a frightened look, grabs Sammy by the hand and drags her to the porch. Yvonne comes out of the house. Nanay Gustia says something to her.

"Samantha! What are you doing out here by yourself?" Her mother asks with panic in her eyes.

"It's OK, mom. I was just following the trail of lizard eggs. See?" She says, pointing at the colorful eggs still on the ground. The last thing she needs is for her mother to raise an alarm. Sammy must remain calm and reveal nothing.

"Are you sure you didn't go up to Tita Milly's house? You didn't go near the mango tree?"

"Mom, can't you see I'm still in my jammies? I was sitting out here writing in my journal when I saw Prieto crunching something in his mouth. I got curious and saw that he was eating lizard eggs. I think someone is playing a joke on us. Anyway, they taste really yummy, just like chocolate covered M&M peanuts. Want one?"

Yvonne explains to Nanay Gustia and the two of them laugh with relief.

"Someone must have liked the lizard egg story a lot," Yvonne says, hugging her daughter tightly.

"Can I sit out here on the porch for a little while? I'm not finished writing and I promise I won't wander off," Sammy says.

"OK, but you have to come in soon and get dressed. The family meeting will be after breakfast," Yvonne says, as she goes back in the house. Nanay Gustia remains outside tending to the garden, but keeps Sammy in her sight.

Lolo Ciano, what am I going to do?

You're going to go on as usual. You cannot let anyone know what's happened. It will create panic.

Should I tell Ollie? Maybe she can help. Oh, but we're leaving tomorrow.

No, you cannot tell anyone. The duwende will find out. Don't forget this is his domain. He will not hesitate to go after your cousins.

Can't I stay here and search for the dwende's new home?

No. The spell has been cast. Go back to San Francisco and wait. There is nothing else we can do now.

Sammy hangs her head.

Don't despair. You must be strong. And stop your hand gesturing. Old woman Gustia is looking at you. She probably thinks you've lost your mind. I have to go. You will be safe for now. Remember, not a word to anyone.

The spirit of Lolo Ciano vanishes.

Chapter 25 ~ The Bait

Sammy gets up and walks back to the house. Her noisy cousins, her parents, aunts and uncles and the smell of breakfast greet her. All of it comforting.

Only Patti stares at her. *What gives, Sam?*

Tita Patti, did you say something?

The look of shock of having uttered her first words of mind talk is all over her aunt's face.

"Oh my," Patti says to herself.

Meanwhile…

Ollie doesn't know if she should be happy or sad. Maybe both. Only one day left of the family's stay on the farm. After a return to San Pablo for a few days, they take the big airplane back to where they live. Who knows when she will see Sammy again?

How can she leave her parents and fly to Germany with Mama Ika, after finally finding out who they are?

That was so happy, so joyous, to find out at last where she belonged after so many years in the orphanage. Ollie instantly felt at home in the little house on stilts by the blue lagoon. She ran through the garden of beautiful flowers, found a creek bubbling merrily behind the thatched house. For the first time in her life, Ollie felt happy and complete.

Daniel and Ligaya told her their story, how they nearly let the *duwende* snatch Sammy's mother Yvonne, when she was a little girl.

"We were lovesick, foolish," Ligaya says, trying to help Ollie understand. "We never wanted anything bad to happen."

Her parents hadn't meant to, but they put Sammy's mother in danger.

Because of Yvonne's narrow escape, Daniel and Ligaya were crazy with fear that the *dwende* might try to take their baby. So they left Ollie on the steps of the orphanage in Manila.

"I cried for days, Ollie," Ligaya said. "I cried until my tears didn't taste salty anymore."

Daniel nodded sadly. "But we knew we would get you back someday, Ollie. You inherited the gift of mind talk from us."

A gift is exactly what it was, a gift from the fairies in the woods.

"We found many fairies in a jar one day when we were deep in the woods," Daniel said. "Some thoughtless children had captured them and left them there. We set them free, and then they gave us the gift of mind talk. It has been passed on to you, my girl."

Ligaya hugged her. "The mind talk was what we used, Ollie, to give you the dreams. You were too little to understand at first, but they are what kept you tied to us."

Ollie remembers the dreams well. Night after night she lay sleeping in the orphanage, dreaming of the thatched house and the garden by the lagoon. She realizes the voices were Daniel and Ligaya, whispering that they loved her and had not forgotten her, that some day they would all be together.

It was all planned from the start. Daniel and Ligaya put the idea in Ollie's mind, and put her in Mama Ika's dream.

"But what about Sammy?" Ollie said. "How does she have mind talk?"

"It's handed down from her grandmother's side," Ligaya said. "A few of them inherited the gift."

Daniel also told her that it was the fairies who provided the light in the jungle for Kuya Bobby and Morris the night they escaped with Yvonne.

"The fairies whisper to us," he said. "They whisper to us of the danger to come, and lately their whispers have become more urgent. The fairies say that Jenny and the *duwende* are working together."

Ollie turns all this over in her mind. She knows she must help her friend. She decides to spy on that creepy Jenny. Ollie suspects Tito Joe is in on it, that Jenny has some power over him.

Somehow, knowing what she must do makes her feel better, but she must do it alone. Her parents would never let her do something so dangerous.

The Family Meeting

It is the last day of the fiesta. The vans are parked down the hill to take the family to San Pablo the next day.

"It will be hard leaving the farm," Patti sighs as she and Sammy walk down the hill to attend the family meeting. "It's not often all ten of us are in one place at the same time. Aside from your Tito John, I am happiest when surrounded by my family."

Sammy grabs her aunt's hand. "Tita Patti, do you remember when you said What gives, Sam? But you really didn't say it? How we just knew it in our minds?"

Patti laughs. "Wasn't that weird? It felt like some form of telepathy. Things like that freak me out."

"Maybe we could practice it, Tita Patti. A secret way to talk? You know, like if we ever had an emergency?"

"Oh, maybe someday, Sam. Come on, we have to hurry. The meeting is about to start. You know how important the clean-up project is to the family and the people who live on the farm."

Sammy follows Patti, disappointed that her aunt won't accept that she has the gift.

The meeting hall is packed with family members and locals. The annual meeting is usually to discuss the

PATRICIA LAUREL

planting season, harvest, repairs and improvements on the farm, but this time the first order of business is the clean-up project.

Sammy listens to her aunts' plan to clean up the bay and the small creek littered with garbage in town. They talk about recycling and putting a stop to illegal fishing. They also discuss a plan to start seaweed and coral farming. The family will finance the project. Eva, the fish girl, and an environmental expert will train the farmers and fishermen. Daniel and Ligaya will be in charge of recycling.

The project will begin immediately. Eva is overjoyed. Maybe there is hope for humans, after all.

The meeting turns to family matters. The locals excuse themselves.

"Does anyone have anything to add before we get on with other farm business?" Morris asks, looking at Jenny.

Surprisingly, Jenny is quiet. This puzzles the others as she is always the first to argue.

Sammy watches Jenny beckon to Tito Joe as she gets up from her chair. She leaves the meeting and heads back to her house. Pretty soon, Tito Joe gets up and goes the same way.

"Mom, can I go back to the house?"

"No, I don't want you going off anywhere by yourself," Yvonne says. "We'll be done soon. If you're feeling antsy, go and join your cousins. Looks like they're having fun playing games with the other kids."

Sammy sighs. She's hardly in the mood to play games. She sees Ollie get up from her chair. Her friend looks at her before leaving.

Sammy! I have to go and do something. I promise we'll talk when I return. I'll tell you everything I know, OK?

Ollie! We need to talk.

Wait for me. I won't be gone long.

Please be careful.

I'll be careful, Sammy.

Ollie waves and heads after Jenny and Tito Joe. Sammy has a bad feeling, but can only wait for her friend's return.

When Things Go From Bad to Worse...

Ollie, behind a tree, listens to Jenny and Joe.

Joe wrings his hands and wipes the sweat from his face. Jenny squints and stares at him harshly, which causes Joe more distress.

"I left a trail of M&Ms from the house to the mango tree," he says. "I didn't stay to see what happened, but I think..."

"Quiet!" Jenny hisses at him.

She catches a glimpse of something behind one of the trees. She pretends to make conversation with Joe, but steals glances from the corner of her eye. It's that pesky girl her cousin Ika picked up at the orphanage, spying on them. Jenny has resented Ollie from the start, the way the family took to her. What if she were to disappear?

"Tito Joe, look over there by the tree!" she suddenly says loudly. "I see a cobra, we'd better get back inside the house right away!"

Frightened, Ollie takes her eyes off Jenny and looks at where the woman pointed. Suddenly a hand clamps over her mouth. She struggles but Jenny holds her tightly.

"What do we do with little children who eavesdrop?" Jenny whispers menacingly in the little girl's ear.

PATRICIA LAUREL

"What are you going to do to her?" Joe asks. "If you hurt her, the deal is off."

"Too late to worry about that now, Tito."

"She's just a child. What harm can she do?"

"Oh, plenty, I'm sure. She and that Sammy are pretty close. I bet she tells her everything. Stay out here and make sure no one is around."

With her hand over the girl's mouth, Jenny heads for her house. Ollie prays that someone who can help her will be in the house, but it is empty. She struggles frantically, kicking, clawing and shouting. She sinks her teeth into Jenny's hand, but she is no match for the older woman.

Jenny drags Ollie inside her bedroom. She stuffs a wad of tissue in Ollie's mouth to prevent the girl from crying out, and ties her hands and feet with tape. Then she locks the door and stands over the girl gloating.

"What am I going to do with you?"

Ollie glares defiantly, trying to shout, but the tissue in her mouth stifles her.

There is a tapping on the window. Jenny sees a basket hat bobbing up and down. She walks over and looks out. There is the *duwende*, impatiently rubbing his hands.

"We need to hide the girl or she will ruin everything. She is the eyes and ears of Sammy. The two of them communicate with their minds," the *duwende* says.

Chapter 27 ~ When Things Go From Bad to Worse...

"They can talk to each other without speaking? How clever," Jenny says.

"There is no time for small talk. Meet me at the fish hatchery. People will think she ran away. Bring her before word gets out that she's missing. Remove the *anting-anting* from her wrist, and silence her before she gets a message out!"

"I'll have Tito Joe take her there now," Jenny says. She sees her uncle in the yard, pacing back and forth, mopping sweat from his face.

Jenny pauses for a moment to watch him and revel in the misery she is causing. Inflicting pain on other people makes her feel important and powerful.

"There is no time to lose! Hurry!" the *duwende* says before vanishing.

Fear numbs Ollie. She has to think fast. The *duwende* and Jenny are in this together. Tito Joe seems to be a reluctant participant. She must get word to Sammy and her parents.

What about her parents and Mama Ika? What will they think when they discover she's missing? She concentrates very hard and screams in her mind.

SAMMY, HELP! TELL MY PARENTS. JENNY, THE *DUWENDE* AND…

Everything goes blank as Jenny takes a heavy book and knocks her unconscious.

Jenny finds a burlap bag and stuffs the little girl inside.

Things happen fast.

She calls Joe and tells him to get his horse and take Ollie to where the *duwende* waits.

Despairing, Joe can do nothing but obey. He is in too deep.

Back at the meeting, Sammy sits beside her mother, writing in her journal. Suddenly the screaming in her mind slams her back against the chair, causing it to almost tip over.

At the same time Ollie fills Sammy's mind with her screams, Patti's head jerks around. She covers her ears and turns to Sammy.

Ollie! What's wrong?

No reply. Sammy calls Ollie's name a few more times in vain. She gets up from the chair.

"Something's happened to Ollie," Sammy says.

"What did you say? How do you know?" Ika asks. All her aunts and Lola gather around her.

Sammy tells them she heard Ollie screaming for help. She thinks it came from the direction of Jenny's house.

"You heard Ollie's scream from there?" Yvonne asks.

"I heard it too," Patti says.

Jenny shows up as they are about to leave. She is out of breath, perspiration glistens on her forehead.

"What's going on?" she asks, beating the air with her fan.

"What did you do? Run from your house?" Mari asks.

"Yes, why?"

"Sammy and I heard Ollie crying for help and it came from the direction of your house," Patti says.

"I don't think so. It's pretty quiet down there. I'm sure I didn't hear anything," Jenny says, looking daggers at Sammy.

"So, you have no idea where Ollie is?" Patti asks

"I came to invite you all to my house for *merienda* this afternoon. I ran because I wanted to catch you before the meeting ends, but instead I get cross examined like a criminal," she says.

"Look," Ika says. "We're sorry if we offended you, but thanks for the invitation. Maybe another day."

Jenny puts on a sympathetic smile and says, "I guess I better get back to the house. I still have to get ready for the other guests. I hope you find Ollie."

She gives Sammy a cold smile and walks away.

"That one is always around every time there is trouble. She lives for it," Milly says.

"C'mon, there is no time to waste. We have to find Ollie," Ika says.

Daniel and Ligaya rush in. They look at Sammy. Ollie's mother uses mind talk.

Sammy! What has happened? We heard Ollie's cry for help! Where is our daughter?

Sammy tells them about Ollie following Jenny and shortly after that, her cry for help.

Oh no! We've waited so long to get our daughter back, only to lose her again. Ligaya crumples to the floor, sobbing. Daniel picks her up and takes her in his arms.

Nanay Gustia rushes in and urgently whispers to Lola.

"Gustia says the spikes have been removed from the *duwende*'s mound," Lola says. "There is nothing to stop him now. Get everyone together at Ika's house. Keep an eye on the children. We must hurry."

They all head back to Ika's house. The older cousins stay outside and watch the younger ones. Sammy goes inside with the adults.

Lola tells them that those with young children should return to San Pablo immediately. "The older ones can stay behind and help look for Ollie."

"Can't Nanay Gustia put the spikes back?" Yvonne asks fearfully.

"No, Gustia's spell is broken. We have no time to waste," Lola says, looking at Milly cradling her grandchild in her arms. "The *duwende*'s power is back."

Chapter 27 ~ When Things Go From Bad to Worse...

"But why did the *dwende* take Ollie?" Mari asks her mother.

Lola looks at them and decides the time has come to tell it all.

"Because she's the daughter of Daniel and Ligaya, and they were very much a part of your father's fight with the *duwende*. The *duwende* lives a long, long time and he never forgets."

She tells her children what happened ten years ago when Ollie was born.

"Daniel and Ligaya came to see me in San Pablo. They were afraid the *duwende* would come after Ollie. We decided to hide her in an orphanage in Manila."

"Don't tell me my picking Ollie to be my foster daughter is a coincidence," Ika says.

"*Hija*, you'll find out soon enough," Lola says. "We have no time to talk now."

"Ika, Milly and I will stay behind to organize a search party. The rest of you leave this afternoon," Morris says.

"Mom, I have to stay here," Sammy says.

Yvonne hugs her daughter tightly. "Sammy, I know Ollie is your friend and you want to help, but we cannot risk it. We must go."

Sammy knows the damage has been done. She will lose her voice as soon as she gets on the plane to San Francisco. Her writing will turn to chicken scratch.

"Sammy?" Patti is standing in front of her. "Tito John and I have decided to stay a few more days on the farm. We won't be flying back with you."

"You can't! You have to come back with us!"

"We must help look for Ollie. For now, nothing is more important."

Sammy fights back desperate tears. As the others are packing and making hurried preparations to depart, she writes in her journal. She writes it all down, hoping she didn't leave anything out — the mind talk, Lolo Ciano, Jenny, how the *duwende* cast a spell on her, everything.

When her parents read the journal, they will know they must find the *duwende* to get her voice back. It is a terrible risk. But she must try. She puts the journal with her backpack in the van.

Sammy sees her cousins milling around in Ika's garden, unsure of what is going on. "Sammy! You were inside. What is going on? We heard Ollie has been kidnapped," Victoria says, running up to her.

"They don't know yet," Sammy says. She does not want to worry her cousins.

It is time to leave, quick goodbyes. Sammy goes to Tito Joe and hugs him.

"I know you're not a bad person. I think you were forced to do something you didn't want to. You need to say something. Please, help us," she whispers in his ear.

Chapter 27 ~ When Things Go From Bad to Worse...

As the vans drive off, Sammy turns around to see Jenny confronting Tito Joe. He waves her off and walks away. Sammy hopes he does the right thing.

Jenny looks after the vans smiling. She doesn't wave. She holds something close to her.

The ride to San Pablo is silent. Even Victoria knows to keep quiet.

Only Sammy talks. She keeps talking and talking. To herself, her parents, Tita Mari, Victoria and Lola who are in the van with her. She talks about the search for Ollie, the beach cleanup, the fiesta. They are not used to Sammy going on about anything and everything.

Poor Sammy, Yvonne thinks. All of this has her so rattled.

Sammy is desperate. She wants to talk and listen to her voice while she still can because soon it will be gone.

At the farm, they look everywhere for Ollie. People from nearby towns who have come for the fiesta leave, dragging their protesting children with them. A pall of fear blankets the farm.

Night comes with still no sign of Ollie. Lights flicker everywhere in the dark accompanied by voices calling out her name. Streaks of bright light zoom in and out of trees as Daniel and Ligaya's fairy friends help search for the lost girl.

The last night of the fiesta is dreary and solemn. The DJ tries in vain to get the handful of die-hard fiesta goers to

PATRICIA LAUREL

dance to his canned music. Only Jenny enjoys herself. She doesn't mind that the food is cold and her drink is warm. She even encourages the people there to have a good time.

Jenny has the doctored deed to the farm that will make her rich. Tomorrow she heads for the city to keep her appointment with the electric company.

She has stolen something else that is precious. She knows Sammy's secrets. Secrets her family will never know.

Jenny touches her forehead. The mole the *duwende* put there is bigger. She shrugs that off, thinking about the villa near Barcelona that she has agreed to buy.

She needs an early start tomorrow. Besides, that Tito Joe is becoming a real nuisance with his worrying. Who cares if he spills his guts? It will be too late.

"But first, a visit to the ocean," she says, holding the journal in her hand tightly as if someone might snatch it from her.

PATRICIA LAUREL

The Trip Home

Sammy feels like a character in a movie. The scene is on fast forward, but no one knows how it ends.

The trip to San Pablo, the call to the airlines to change their departure date and last minute things to tend to, all happening in fast forward.

Until the moment they board the airplane, Sammy yaks away.

The plane is airborne. The flight attendant asks if she wants something to drink. She nods and begins to say apple juice, but no words come. Sammy points to the can of juice.

The attendant pours her apple juice.

Sammy pulls her backpack from under the seat and looks in it.

The journal is gone!

The little girl sobs, as her mother tries to comfort her.

"Oh, Sammy," Yvonne says. "Don't worry, they'll find Ollie, and things will be better when we get home."

She can't tell her mother that things will get worse. Sammy cannot say a word.

Back to the Present

In San Francisco with Sammy and Lolo Ciano…

I'm so glad to see you, Lolo Ciano! Where have you been? Are you here to help me? Oh, please, please. I'm in so much trouble!

Sammy's great-great-great uncle stands by the fireplace, avoiding the traffic of people in the living room.

I've been looking for the duwende's new home.

Wow, I'm so glad you and I can still communicate. I tried to reach Tita Patti, but no luck. Everything comes out garbled. She calls it radio static.

Sammy thinks back to their arrival at the San Francisco airport a few days ago. It was not noticeable during the flight. She pretended to sleep to avoid talking.

She got away with shrugging, shaking and nodding her head, walking down the ramp to baggage claim. For a little while. Of course, it was Victoria who had to say that something was not right.

"Mom, I've been talking to Sammy this whole time, but she won't talk to me!"

"What? Is it because you're a nag? Maybe that's why she's not talking to you," Mari said. "Maybe Sammy's just tired. Why don't you leave her alone?"

"But, Mom! I think there is something wrong with Sammy," Victoria insisted.

Oh, oh… Sammy thought. Victoria's concern attracted her parents' attention. They approached her.

A gentle pat on the shoulder brings her back to the present.

I'm sorry, Lolo Ciano. I was just thinking about the day I lost my voice. What were you saying?

I was saying that the duwende can only cast spells on humans. He has no power over spirits, but we are still going to need help finding him. First, let's listen to what is being said here.

"So, what did the *manghuhula* have to say?" Yvonne asks Mari.

"Nothing really concrete, except that Sammy is being tormented by a creature from the earth. You know, an enchanted being," Mari says.

"The *duwende*," Yvonne says fearfully.

The phone rings. Yvonne goes to pick it up.

It is Patti in Honolulu.

Everyone listens to Yvonne's uh huhs and huhs. She barely says a word.

"We're flying to Honolulu," she says, looking at her daughter. "Patti says to tell Sammy she's been having some very disturbing dreams. Something to do with the *duwende*."

"She also says that Sammy needs to be with Solo now. It is very important that we leave right away. She and John arrived from Manila this morning."

Sammy looks at Lolo Ciano.

Yes, Samantha. Solo has the help we need now. He may know what to do.

"Victoria and I will come with you," Mari says. "I'll worry about the expense later. You start packing and I'll take care of the tickets."

The phone rings again. Jack picks it up.

"OK. I'll tell them," he says grimly. "That was Larry. A lawyer representing an electric company showed up at the farm claiming possession. The company apparently has a deed of sale with everyone's signature. Guess who sold the farm?"

"Jenny," Mari says. "It looks like Honolulu will only be a layover. We definitely have to go home."

"Larry has booked a flight," Jacks says. "He leaves tomorrow with Robert, Mike and Marc. He says that heavy machine equipment is standing by to bulldoze a path to the beach. That is where they plan to build a power plant."

"Any more bad news?" Yvonne asks, tears in her eyes.

"He says that Tito Joe hasn't been seen for days. He told his wife that he couldn't face the family."

Chapter 29 ~ Back to the Present

"Sammy said something about Tito Joe being in trouble," Yvonne says.

Sammy sees her father's eyes go wide.

"Oh man!" Jack smacks himself on the forehead. "Yvonne," he says, "remember the night before we flew to Manila? Sammy had that strange dream about the little man with the long beard and the man in white. She mentioned other things, but I forget what they were. Am I right?"

"The *duwende* is the little man," Yvonne says.

"It's funny. I dreamed about it last night. I dreamed about Sammy's dream, that is," Jack says.

"Who is the man in white?" Victoria asks.

"I think only Sammy has the answer to that," Jack says.

Did you do that with my dad's dream, Lolo Ciano? Sammy asks.

Yes, I did. I concentrated on your father because your mother's mind is a jumble of confusion and fear. It would not have worked on her. Your father is more focused.

Mari holds up her cell phone. "I've booked a flight to leave tomorrow morning for Honolulu, and then we fly to Manila the next day."

Lolo Ciano, I guess the images I put in Tita Patti's dream worked. Since I lost my voice, I've been concentrating hard to get a message in her dreams.

We will see. Your friend Solo needs to come with us, but I think he already knows it.

I get it. We are going to fight magic with magic. Solo's eyes can help find the duwende and his hiding place.

Yes, Samantha, but you need to stop gesturing with your hands. You are alarming your parents.

Sammy puts her hands at her side.

"Sam," Yvonne says. "Kiss Tita Mari and Victoria goodbye. Thank goodness, we're traveling light this time."

Yvonne prays this nightmare will end. She wants her daughter back.

"Sammy, don't worry. I'll do the talking for you," Victoria says gently.

Sammy hugs her cousin.

That night, Yvonne looks in on her sleeping daughter. Tears rush down her cheeks as she lovingly plants a kiss on Sammy's head. An invisible hand touches her shoulder. She shivers as if a cold breeze made her spine tingle.

Lolo Ciano wishes he could do more. *I have to go now, Samantha. I cannot linger. There are other things that must be done.*

Satisfied that Sammy will receive his message in her dreams, the spirit of the man in white departs.

The next day Jack, the two sisters and their daughters arrive in Honolulu. Waiting at the airport are Patti and John and the old man with the shining eyes.

30

Back at the Farm...

Ollie feels along the wall of the prison that holds her. Solid rock. She had thought the *duwende*'s home would have more of an earthy feel, like the burrow of some animal. This cannot be his home by the mango tree.

Of course! She's been taken somewhere else. The mound would be the first place her parents would look.

One hand is chained to the wall. It is so dark that she might as well be blindfolded. She tries using mind talk, but it's no use. Her words bounce off the rock.

She has not seen or heard the *duwende*. The last thing she remembers is Jenny whispering threats in her ear, and then waking up here in darkness.

At least the *duwende* left her food and water. Jenny would probably have left her to starve.

"Oh, please, please. Someone help me!" she cries desperately.

Nobody hears her.

Eva, the fish girl, is underwater. She should be with the others helping to look for missing Ollie. She feels a tinge of guilt. But today she needs a little time alone with her thoughts. She lingers in the water.

PATRICIA LAUREL

She is full of fear. The clean-up project is on hold. Sea creatures are seriously threatened, as well as people who depend on the ocean for their living.

Huge, menacing bulldozers are at the farm's boundary, ready to move in.

She swims to the bottom and looks around the ocean floor. The spot she swims to is littered with garbage. She picks up the smaller pieces she can take up to the surface.

If only people understood. The sea gives so much, but if it dies, everything will be taken away.

Eva is about to swim away when the bright pink color attracts her attention. She swims toward it. She finds it curious that someone took the trouble to make sure the plastic case does not float up to surface by tying it to a concrete slab. Something is inside. She takes it with her.

Back on shore, she joins the search for Ollie.

It is almost dark when Eva and her grandmother return home. Another day of fruitless searching.

Eva is so tired; she does not bother to eat supper. She flops down on the *banig* mat on the floor. She is drifting toward sleep when she sees the plastic case. She picks up the case and opens it.

There is a notebook inside. In big letters are the words "SAMANTHA PLUM".

She jumps from her bed and shouts for her grandmother.

"LOLA!"

"What is it? You're going to wake the fish with your screaming," her grandmother says, rushing in from the porch.

"Look at this," she explains to her grandmother where she found the journal.

"Quickly, now," Nanay Gustia says. "We need to dry some of the pages."

After the pages dry, Nanay Gustia wraps the journal in several plastic bags and secures it with rubber bands.

"Eva, go now and summon a fish with authority. Send Sammy's journal to a man called Solo who lives in Hawai'i. Patti told me of this man whose ancestral spirit is the tiger shark. The shark will know what to do."

"How do I persuade a fish from our waters to travel that far? And what if it doesn't get to this man in time?"

"Child, don't stand here asking questions. Talk to the fish. Tell them about the power plant."

Eva goes to the starry shore. She swims out of the bay and into the China Sea. She dives underwater and calls out.

A huge white bulk appears, circles her, and inspects her. Eva has seen this kind before, but this is the biggest great white shark she has ever encountered.

She summons her courage and begins to talk.

The shark is motionless. Eva places the journal gently in the enormous teeth.

Eva watches the great white speed gracefully away. She feels that the fish had been expecting her plea for help. She hopes it is not too late.

This is how Solo's *aumakua* received help from the great white shark to transport Sammy's journal between the Philippine islands and the Hawaiian islands. Like the pony express, the journal passes from one shark to the next, even speedy dolphins help out, until it reaches the mouth of the tiger shark waiting by the shores of Kailua, Oʻahu.

PATRICIA LAUREL

31

The Island of O'ahu

Once again on a flight from San Francisco to Honolulu, but this time it is Sammy and her parents, her cousin Victoria and her mother, Mari. They are on their way to pick up Patti and Solo, who will fly with them to Manila.

With Victoria sitting by her side, Sammy reflects on everything that's happened since their return from the Philippines.

Tita Patti's frantic call telling them to come to Honolulu at once. She says she's got bits and pieces of the puzzle. It came to her in dreams. Tita Patti knows the *duwende* and Jenny are behind all the troubles, and Solo needs to see Sammy.

Jenny, it seems, has fled the Philippines. No one has been able to track her down, and Tito Joe is nowhere to be found.

Ollie is still missing. Is she in the clutches of the *duwende*? Why can't Ollie send her a message using mind talk?

Patti and John meet them at the airport. Solo is with them.

Sammy runs to Solo.

"I told you we would see each other again," Solo says, wrapping Sammy in his arms.

"I just got back yesterday from Manila," Patti says, greeting them. "And tomorrow I'm flying right back. I don't even have time to get over my jet lag!"

"How you holding up, Sam?" Patti hugs Sammy tightly and whispers in her ear, "Think of this as an adventure, kiddo. We're the good guys seeking out the evildoers and crushing them. We have a few bumps along the way, but in the end we will win, right?"

Sammy gives her aunt another big hug.

"I hope you aren't too tired because we have errands to run before your early flight tomorrow," John says. "Our first stop is Chinatown. We'll eat dim sum there and Solo has to pick up a few things. After that, we drive to Kailua for an early supper at Solo and Nani's house and later to the beach for the moonrise. We'll have time to talk about what to do."

"What's a moonrise? I thought there were only sunrises," Victoria says.

"You'll see. It's brilliant," Patti says.

"You guys are traveling light this time," John says, loading the van. Soon they are going down Nimitz Highway.

"Honolulu's Chinatown is not as big as the one in San Francisco, but it's just as interesting and mysterious, especially at night," John says, as he pulls into a parking garage.

They walk through streets jammed with fried rice stands and soup stalls, Asian groceries, lei sellers, curio shops, sailor bars, tattoo parlors, fruit and vegetable stands. Smoked ducks, garlands of flowers, and ropes of onion and garlic hang in the shops.

John leads them through an indoor food court crowded with people. The smell is heavenly and tempting.

They leave the aroma of food behind and follow John down a few steps into another section of the building. The shoppers' pathway is the only available space.

Sammy is fascinated. She listens to the bantering and haggling in Mandarin, Vietnamese, Tagalog and Korean.

"I'm sure we're ready to eat dim sum. What do you think, Sammy?" Patti asks.

They climb some creaky stairs to Wo Fat's restaurant, overlooking Hotel Street. Soon they are crowded into a booth, ordering from waitresses who cruise through the tables pushing carts and announcing their varieties of dim sum: steamed and baked buns, shumai, pot stickers, fried fish balls, shrimp and spring rolls.

"Sammy, we'll have to learn how to use chopsticks. That way we can eat slower," Victoria says, attacking one dish after another with her fork.

"Chicken feet," Solo says, "let's have some chicken feet."

Victoria makes a face.

After the meal, they leave the restaurant and follow John and Solo to the Oahu Market on King Street.

"Your uncle is with us today," Solo whispers to Sammy, pointing his thumb behind him.

She looks around and sees Lolo Ciano inspecting the sign above a storefront. It says Herbs and Acupuncture.

"You forget, *keiki*. I have the gift of sight. I see things that most people can't see. I can see the ghosts of Chinatown right now, as we walk. Your uncle is one of them. And no, I cannot talk to him like you do."

Sammy greets her great-great-great uncle with a smile. Lolo Ciano walks through the door of the shop.

Sammy and Solo take the lead, and the others follow them into the Herbs and Acupuncture store. Lolo Ciano is standing by a red curtain at the rear of the store.

The store is small and they barely fit in the center, surrounded by glass cases. The walls are covered with shelves from floor to ceiling full of all sorts of glass jars and tin cans labeled in Chinese.

Solo greets the owner and introduces his friends.

"This is my friend Yi Fan. He specializes in acupuncture, healing herbs and tea from China, as well as other things," Solo says.

Solo's friend bows politely and smiles at Sammy. He wears a light, gray mandarin collared jacket over matching trousers. He's about Solo's age. He has a neatly trimmed goatee and smells of the herbs he sells. Yi Fan leans over and whispers to Solo, "This is the bewitched child, my old friend?"

Yi Fan treats them to his special tea brewing on a mini stove. It tastes very refreshing. Lolo Ciano nods and steps to one side as Solo and Yi Fan go behind the red curtain. They return in a few minutes, Solo carries a small brown paper bag.

Solo tells them he purchased Yi Fan's special herbs. He says his Chinese friend is the only one who knows its ingredients. "It will come in handy when we hunt for the *duwende*," he says.

They say goodbye to Yi Fan and walk back to the parking garage.

Sammy sees Lolo Ciano ahead, beckoning her to follow him. She tugs at her mother's sleeves.

"Wait up. I think Sammy wants us to follow her," Yvonne says.

Sammy follows Lolo Ciano. They stop at one of the lei stands. Sammy picks out a lei strand of white plumeria.

They follow Sammy across Beretania Street to a small plaza by the river. In a small promenade, beside the Chinese Cultural Center are bronze statues of Dr. Jose Rizal and Dr. Sun Yat-Sen, national heroes of their countries, the Philippines and China.

Sammy notices that Dr. Rizal has a very serious and resolute look on his face, as if he is ready to face the firing squad.

"How could Sammy know about these statues?" Yvonne asks, and answers the question herself. "Never mind, nothing surprises me anymore."

In front of Rizal's statue are a half-dozen old Filipino men, veterans of the Bataan Death March during World War II. They are bent and old, creaky and frail, in their campaign caps and medals. Several lean on canes. They drape the statue with leis.

"These old guys come here all the time," John says. "Every once in a while the *Advertiser* runs a story about them, how they fought with the resistance against the Japanese, and how they come here to honor Rizal in remembrance of those who died for the Philippines."

When they see Sammy approaching timidly with her white plumeria lei, the old men smile and make a place for her.

Jack and John hold her up, and she places her lei around the neck of the national hero, her ancestor.

Lolo Ciano stands off to one side, stiffly at attention, beaming.

The family stands in front of their ancestor's statue for a few minutes. All lost in their own thoughts, asking for help with the troubles they face.

I wish Tita Patti could see you, Lolo Ciano. If she can mind talk, she should be able to see you, right?

Don't worry. She'll see me soon enough. She's still trying to come to terms with the gift handed down to her. Let her deal with that first. She hasn't opened herself up to accept it, but it will happen.

One of the old men starts whispering excitedly and points to the statue.

"Look," he says to Yvonne, who is holding Sammy's hand. "Look."

On the bronze face of Jose Rizal, Yvonne sees the beginning of a smile.

When they leave for the parking garage, Sammy looks back one more time. The old men salute the statue.

They drive out of the city via the scenic Pali Highway to Kailua. They pass sheer green cliffs with rivulets of waterfalls, miles of white, sandy beaches and booming, blue surf.

Sammy turns around to see Patti alone in the back seat, deep in thought. Her aunt does not see Lolo Ciano sitting beside her.

Solo's daughter Nani greets them. They eat an early supper, and then off to the beach to view the sunset and full moon rising.

As they remove their shoes and walk across the sand, Patti says to her sisters, "There's something you need to know about Sammy and me."

Solo beams and nods. "It's about time you talked about your gift," he says, hugging her.

"Sammy and I can speak to each other with our minds," Patti says. "Daniel, Ligaya and Ollie can do it too. Sammy has dreams, she sees spirits, she sees so much more than I do. I've had this realization about it all along, but I have been resisting it because it scared me so much."

"Well, it is scary," says Yvonne.

"I know," Patti says. "But I feel so guilty. I feel like if I had found the courage to deal with it, maybe Ollie wouldn't have disappeared, and Sammy wouldn't have lost her voice. I never told any of you, not even John, because I was too afraid to face it."

"How did you get the gift, Tita Patti?" Victoria asks. "And why don't I have it?"

Despite themselves, all the sisters laugh.

"I think it's handed down from generation to generation to some of us in the family," Patti says. "I have been having dreams where our ancestor Lolo Ciano comes to us and is trying to help us. I sensed his presence that day we visited the *Bahay na Bato* and Sammy went into a trance when we were standing in the dining room. I should have tried harder then to get in touch with Lolo Ciano. Why didn't I?"

Sammy looks around to see if Lolo Ciano will appear to her aunt, but he is not there. Maybe it's not the right time.

"Lolo Ciano? Whom are you talking about?" Yvonne asks. But before Patti can reply, Yvonne and Mari both say, "You mean Paciano Rizal?"

"I knew you guys would get it. Sammy can see his spirit and talk with him. Lolo Ciano has the gift. Don't even ask me how, but I sense he is here because the family is in trouble," Patti says.

"Have you seen him?" Yvonne asks, startled.

"No. Maybe he's upset with me for not having had the guts to help Sam," Patti says.

John goes to his wife and hugs her. "No one's blaming you. We'll help her now. Everything will work out, Patti, you'll see."

Solo reminds them that time is getting short; the sun is about to go down. He leads the way to the seashore.

Locals and tourists are sitting or walking on the beach. Everyone is waiting for a double feature of the sun setting and a full moon rising. Sammy feels like she is part of a large audience in a concert hall.

Solo points to the twin islands of Mokulua.

"*Moku* means small island and *Lua* means twin or pair. The islands are a sanctuary for birds. People can visit, but they can only walk on the beach so as not to disturb the birds' homes, like the plovers who nest in burrows like rabbits do," Solo explains.

"Watch now," he says.

The sunset is dreamlike, so magical, first the boiling rise of red, yellow and orange, then the slow shimmer of melting light as the sun drowns in the blue sea.

Solo's eyes sparkle.

"He is here," he whispers in Sammy's ear.

As the daylight fades, a white light begins to peek from behind the twin islands, and slowly, it rises as if ascending from the depths of the ocean.

They sit quietly on the sand, and the full moon gradually emerges casting a soft, white glow on the planet Earth. Little bits of sparkle, like jewels glinting, dot the wet part of the beach where the swell of the ocean rushes in and out.

First there is silence, then oohs and the aahs as they look up at the huge, round moon shining over them.

"It's like magic," Yvonne whispers.

Sammy sees the shimmering presence of Lolo Ciano by her side, and Patti staring in disbelief. Magic is indeed all around.

"My *aumakua* is near. He has brought us something important," Solo says.

"What's an *aumakua*?" Victoria asks, looking around.

"Yes, Solo, tell us about your *aumakua*," Patti says. She is trying hard to keep her voice normal.

"My *aumakua* is the tiger shark. It is the spirit of my ancestor who protects my family members and me. I was baptized in the shark's cove. My grandfather took me out in a canoe when I was just a *keiki* and dipped me in the ocean.

You cannot see it from here; it is on the back side of the twin islands.

"I remember it all so clearly, dangling in the ocean as my grandfather's strong arms held me just below the surface. I could look up through the blue water and see my grandfather's face, leaning over the side of the canoe, smiling down at me. My *aumakua* glided up to me, all eyes and teeth. I smiled and blew bubbles at him. The shark god was so happy to see me.

"Since then, the ocean and all who dwell there have been good to me and my family."

The beach is almost empty. Solo gets up and motions the others to follow him to the shore. He has a flashlight.

Something long, dark and sleek swims close to the shore.

"Solo, look! Is that your *aumakua*?" Victoria asks, pointing excitedly as a fin roils the white water in the moonlight.

"Stand back," Solo says, wading out into the surf. "My *aumakua* does not know you. He shows no mercy to those not under his protection."

He stops inches from the tiger shark, bends down and runs his hand on the sleek body, soothing it with his whispers. An object pops up from the water, and Solo catches it. He whispers to his *aumakua* one more time.

They all watch the shark turn away from Solo, then watch as its fin disappears.

The others stand there open mouthed. "Good God," Jack says, "did you see that?"

Solo gives the object to Sammy. She pulls on the rubber bands securing the many plastic bags used to wrap it. The familiar bright pink peeks out.

She runs to her mother and gives her the journal. Yvonne takes it.

They stand on the beach, reading Sammy's journal with a flashlight.

"There's a note from Eva, the fish girl," Yvonne says. "Could she have sent this to us somehow?"

"Read on. She says she found Sammy's journal while she was picking up trash in the ocean," Mari says.

Sammy reaches up and turns the pages to the entry where she met Solo.

"I guess she wants us to start reading here," Mari says.

They read everything. Starting with Solo and the eclipse, the first time Sammy discovers mind talk and meets Ollie, her visit to the past and meeting Lolo Ciano, Jenny's attempt to lure Sammy to the *duwende*'s mound and finally her being caught by the *duwende*. If not for Lolo Ciano coming to her rescue, Sammy would have vanished underground, but the *duwende* was able to cast a spell and take Sammy's voice. She can get her voice back only if she can find the creature of the earth.

PATRICIA LAUREL

Yvonne reads out loud one of Sammy's last entries. "OLLIE, what is wrong? Where are you?"

"Does this mean the *duwende* has Ollie?" Mari asks.

"That's what I have been afraid of all along," Jack says, picking up Sammy and hugging her tightly.

"I think we're prepared to face the *duwende* now," Solo says.

PATRICIA LAUREL

32

Showdown Time

Lola greets them at the airport in Manila. The mood is somber, unlike a few weeks ago when they arrived for the happy family reunion.

Sammy is surprised at the change in Lola. She looks worn out; her shoulders are stooped, as if in defeat.

"I am so relieved to see you. I have never felt so helpless. Oh, where are my manners? You must be Solo. Samantha and Patti have told me about you," Lola says, extending her hand.

"Don't worry. We will find this creature that's been after your granddaughter," Solo says, taking Lola's hand.

Once in the van, Lola fills them in on everything that's been happening on the farm.

"Joe finally showed himself and confessed to his part in Sammy's enchantment and Ollie's disappearance. He wants to join in the search for the *duwende*."

"What do we do about him?" Mari asks.

"We forgive him. He is your father's brother and very much a part of the family. He was in trouble and made a mistake, that's all," Lola says.

"Where are we going, Lola?" Victoria asks.

"We're going to the farm straightaway. There is no time to lose. Sammy, Ollie and the farm need all our help now," Lola says.

"OK. Our turn. I'm too wound up. Solo, will you tell our mother?" Yvonne says.

Solo shows Lola Sammy's journal and explains what it all means.

"Is Lolo Ciano here with us?" Lola asks. Sammy's grandmother accepts the spirit's presence as a natural occurrence.

Solo shakes his head.

"We're not saving the farm only for ourselves. I couldn't bear to think of families being displaced and forced to move to the slums of Manila," Lola says tearfully. "Your father would never forgive us."

"Don't worry, mom. We'll sort this all out. We won't let anything happen to the people or the farm," Mari says.

The trip to the farm seems unbearably long to Sammy. There is no excitement, only apprehension and fear.

They stop at a seaside restaurant for lunch; Solo and Sammy walk to the shore to stretch their travel weary bodies before getting back in the van.

"It is like Hawai'i, and yet it isn't," Solo says to Sammy. "I feel the ground groaning from too many years of abuse. The earth creatures are not happy."

As they walk back to the van, Sammy sees Solo approach Lola. He says something to her, as if to reassure her. Lola clutches Solo's hand with a look of desperate hope in her eyes.

PATRICIA LAUREL

33

Doubts

"This cannot be good," the *duwende* mutters, covering his ears. The rumbling of big machinery gathering above ground can be heard deep beneath the earth where he reigns. He did not think things would turn out this way.

He flees from the noise, which is so powerful it sends tremblings deep into the ground, and finally finds refuge not far from the rock where he keeps Ollie prisoner. At least here, he is safe for a while. That Jenny is responsible for what's happening. Why did he not see it coming? His thirst for revenge blinded him to what Jenny had in mind.

Things are not going his way. The other earth creatures will surely blame him for this.

He was so sure of his plan. What he didn't take into account was Jenny's greed for money and the spirit ancestor of the family.

"Come already. Find me and let's put an end to this," he says, looking up at the ceiling of his underground shelter.

PATRICIA LAUREL

And in the End...

It is mid afternoon and the search for Ollie is not going well. Day after day they search in the tangled jungle and the broiling sun.

The family asked the mayor and the chief of police to keep the workers and their machinery from entering the farm, at least temporarily. If they don't find Ollie and the *duwende* soon, all will be lost.

They are now halfway to the beach and still nothing. Daniel suggests a different route. He leads them past the fish hatchery and into a dense wooded area. It is part of the farm that was never developed. They walk single file on the narrow trail. People are afraid to wander in these parts. It is said to be full of enchanted creatures.

The searchers swat insects in the heat, keeping an eye out for cobras. All have the same thought, but none dare speak it. "We could look forever."

They come to a clearing. There is a creek nearby and a large boulder beside it. Sitting on top of the boulder is a bamboo spout with dripping water.

Daniel goes to the boulder and whispers something to it.

"Ligaya and I are mindful of the one who lives here and I have asked permission to drink the water," he says, holding the spout for anyone wishing a drink.

Sammy drinks from the spout. She places her hand on the boulder for support. Suddenly she has an overwhelming feeling that her friend is nearby.

Ollie, where are you? I can feel you!

No reply.

Sammy goes to Solo and tugs at his shirtsleeve. She points at the boulder.

Solo looks intently at the boulder. "You're right, Sammy. I sense something there, but I don't know what it is. The rock is too solid."

Morris suggests that they turn back and continue the search the next day. He does not like the atmosphere here, and he can see that his mother and Nanay Gustia are worn out.

"No, no, let's keep looking," Jack says.

"We cannot give up. Daniel and I will stay here. I feel our daughter is nearby," Ligaya says, looking at Sammy.

"There is still plenty of light," Lola says, wiping her brow. "It won't be dark for a few hours yet."

Sammy sees Solo's eyes suddenly begin to sparkle. "There!" he says.

Solo pulls a pouch from his pocket and sprinkles the contents of his special herbs on a clump of new dirt that is barely visible on the ground.

"Hurry now. Hold hands and gather around this fresh mound," Solo says. "We will defeat magic with magic. He cannot get away now."

The others watch as Solo, Sammy, Patti, Nanay Gustia, Eva, Daniel and Ligaya approach the mound, holding hands. There is an empty space between Sammy and Patti, but their hands are outstretched, as if holding on to something invisible.

Slowly the air takes on a brightness, a glitter.

"Look!" Lola exclaims.

The space between Sammy and Patti shimmers in the air. Lolo Ciano makes his appearance, holding hands with his nieces.

Everyone can see him, and is astonished, but before they can speak, the mound opens up.

Kicking and screaming, the *duwende* emerges. The hole immediately closes behind him and the culprit is exposed. He looks at the circle of people around him, all of them hostile, menacing.

Brave to the end, he gathers his nerves, squats on the ground and clutches his cutlass. "So, Spirit," the *duwende* says to Lolo Ciano. "Here we are at last, where all can see us."

"So we are, *duwende*," Lolo Ciano says, giving Sammy's hand a squeeze.

The *duwende* stands erect, holding his cutlass, and for a moment Sammy is fearful. Then the *duwende* makes a courtly bow and hands the cutlass to Lolo Ciano.

The spell is broken, and the *duwende*'s magic is undone. When it all unravels, several things happen simultaneously…

On the outskirts of Barcelona, Jenny is with a real estate agent inspecting a villa that she has absolutely fallen in love with. The agent, sleek and prosperous, has a $100 haircut, dark glasses, capped teeth and a gold wristwatch. Jenny carries a briefcase that holds a check for the full payment. She will live in style in her beloved Spain.

"This a lot of money to part with, but I still have lots left," she says to the agent, taking the check out. He gives her an oily smile. Life is good.

She is about to hand the check over when it crumbles into a swirl of dust and blows away. Suddenly the mole on her forehead begins to burn like a hot coal and she shrieks, clutching her head.

The panicked agent calls for an ambulance. The crazed woman writhes and thrashes on the floor, mumbling the word *duende, duende, duende*. The agent does not understand why this woman keeps repeating the Spanish word for elf, and does not care. His fat commission is gone.

The ambulance arrives. The agent is angry that the sale has gone bad. When asked if Jenny has any relatives, he gives the name of Jenny's hotel.

"I know of no relatives. She should be taken to a hospital for the crazy people," he says, locking the door of the house and driving away in his Mercedes.

Because there is no one to claim her, Jenny is placed in an institute for the mentally handicapped. She is assigned a bed in a ward for welfare patients. Still kicking and screaming, she is strapped to the bed and sedated.

Later, the mole on Jenny's forehead disappears along with her memory. She wakes up delirious, not remembering who she is. She jabbers in Spanish, leaving the doctors mystified.

Perhaps the agent, after getting over the loss of the huge commission, will feel pity and give the hospital the background information forms Jenny filled out.

In Manila, the lawyer representing the electric company takes out the proof of sale for the farm from his safe. He looks it over again. Before his disbelieving eyes, the ink gathers and turns to one big blotch in the middle of the paper.

He places a call to his client. No one will believe what has happened, so he says the deed of sale is bogus and will not stand in any court of law. That is all. Payment to Jenny's bank account is stopped.

Back at the farm, a man is on his way home from a hard day's work harvesting coconuts. He walks by Milly's house and sees the mound beside the mango tree slowly go flat, hissing like a leaky balloon. It's as if the mound was never there. He scratches his head and quickly walks away.

Chapter 34 ~ And in the End...

The supervisor of the work crew receives a call on his cell phone. He is ordered to remove the men and machinery from the farm.

As the *duwende* stands in the midst of Sammy's family and friends, the huge boulder breaks in two and Ollie stands there, blinking at the sunlight.

"Ollie!" Daniel sweeps his daughter up and hugs her fiercely. "Oh, Ollie we were afraid we had lost you again!"

He hands her over to the weeping Ligaya, who acts like she will squeeze the breath out of her. "Oh, Ollie," she cries, "Oh, my Ollie!"

Sammy dances around them. Lola and the aunts dab at tears, but the uncles are all staring coldly at the *duwende*.

The *duwende* knows he is defeated.

All eyes are on him now. All is silent and still.

The *duwende* rises, reaches out and touches Sammy on the lips. He steps back when he sees Morris and his brothers closing in on him, their fists clenched. Morris picks up a heavy stick.

"You will not hurt her again, *duwende*!" Morris shouts.

Lolo Ciano holds up his hand. Morris and his brothers stop in their tracks.

"No," he says, "it's not our way."

The brothers back off.

"*Duwende*, have you undone your spell?" Lolo Ciano asks.

"Yes, spirit. It is undone, I know when I am beaten. Now let me go in peace and I promise never to disturb this family again," the *duwende* says.

"It's not that simple. You have to pay for what you've done!" Yvonne shouts.

"MOM!"

Yvonne stops cold. "Sammy said something!"

Jack snatches Sammy up. "Talk to me!" he shouts. "Sammy, talk to me!"

Yvonne throws her arms around them both as Sammy says over and over, "I'm OK now, I'm OK. I can talk. I'm OK."

The family dances happily, deep in the coconut jungle, in the clearing by the bubbling creek.

Amidst all this rejoicing, Lola motions for Solo. They go to Lolo Ciano and talk for a few minutes.

"I speak for my family and I think they will agree," Lola turns to the *duwende*. "Banishing you from the farm is not a solution. You said you have lived here since the Spanish. We need to live with each other.

The *duwende* lowers his head.

"I propose a home for you away from people. You have to pick a new location. Some place where there is little foot traffic. Right here would be a good place. Daniel can build a fence so people will know not to trespass."

"That is a very good solution," the *duwende* says with much relief. "I agree to your proposal. In return, here is something to help with your clean-up project and improvements."

He hands something to Lola.

"Oh my goodness! Is this what I think it is?" Lola asks, holding up the object for everyone to see.

"In my travels underground, I sometimes find precious things," the *duwende* says, smiling.

In Lola's hand is the biggest ruby they have ever seen.

"Wow! Do you know how much that gem is worth? Lots!" Mike says.

"What about Jenny? Will she cause any more trouble?" Yvonne asks.

"You will not be hearing from that one for a long while. If and when she does show up, she won't be causing any more trouble," the *duwende* says.

It is time for him to leave. He bows to Lola and her family. "I will always remember this day, Doña Marita. I have learned a valuable lesson from you."

He looks at Sammy.

"Samantha, if you think we can be friends after what I've done, it would very much please me," the *duwende* says, holding out his hand to Sammy. "I hope your mother can forgive me."

"It's done with," Yvonne says.

"Mr. *Duwende*, maybe we can be friends," Sammy says, taking his hand. "Maybe we could stay in touch through Ollie."

The *duwende* doffs his basket hat, makes a sweeping bow, smiles and disappears into the earth.

Joe, who has been hanging back, finally musters the courage to speak.

"Thank God," he says, "thank God all of Jenny's stupid plans failed." He looks down at the ground. "Can all of you forgive me someday?"

"Of course we can, Joe," Lola says quickly.

Chapter 34 ~ And in the End...

[286]
PATRICIA LAUREL

Bittersweet

The next morning, they are ready to head back to the States.

Sammy and Ollie say goodbye, but there is no sadness because they will see each other again. Ollie will live with her parents at last. She hugs her friend and they promise to communicate via mind talk or the old fashion way, by mail.

Victoria insists. "But you have to tell me what you say to each other. You can't leave me out. I must know."

Sammy says goodbye to Daniel and Ligaya, Nanay Gustia and Eva.

Sammy and her family know that the farm will be in good hands. They will be there to help Tito Joe and the other relatives.

It is Lolo Ciano's time to depart, and he wants to give the family a special present.

The family stand together in the yard before Milly's house, not far from the mango tree.

"Samantha, take your Tita Patti's hand, and together we can concentrate hard. Patti, what has been your most fervent wish? Think about it and let's see what happens," Lolo Ciano says, using regular speech. Now that the family can see him, there is no need for mind talk.

With all their might, they concentrate hard. Patti wishing that she could hug her father; Sammy hoping to meet her grandfather; and Lola wishing that her husband could know that everyone is safe and the farm is secure.

At first they do not see the figure emerging from behind the mango tree.

Handsome and robust, the man with a smile that lights up a room, walks toward his family.

Lola utters a cry of surprise. The children look at their mother and follow her gaze.

"Pappy!" All his children cry out simultaneously. At first they hesitate, not sure whether to get close. Then Milly runs to him.

"Pappy, can we touch you?" Milly asks apprehensively.

"Please, *hija*," he tells her, opening his arms.

Cries and tears of joy engulf him. He looks at his wife and smiles. His children open the circle for their mother. They watch their parents greet each other, all hands on their father, afraid of letting him go.

"There is something I have to do first," he tells them.

Standing a few feet away, Joe bows his head, ashamed to look at his older brother. If he could make himself disappear, he would do it.

PATRICIA LAUREL

"*Kuya* Bobby, I am so sorry. I broke my promise to you, our siblings and most of all, our parents," Joe says to his brother standing before him.

"Joe, always remember the family will be here for you. Trust yourself to turn to them when you are in need," Bobby says.

The two brothers hug. "Go to your family. They have missed you for years," Joe says, wiping the tears from his face.

Sammy feels the joy all around her. She and Victoria are content to watch Lolo with his children. The aunts update him on their lives and the uncles discuss the planting and harvest season with their father.

Sammy walks over to where Lolo Ciano and Solo are. She dreads saying good-bye to her great-great-great uncle.

"Samantha, don't be sad. I have a feeling that we will have other adventures," Lola Ciano says.

"And you can come and visit me, *keiki*," Solo says. "I can show you Hawai'i."

The reunion ends all too soon. It is time for their father to leave the earth and rejoin his spirit family. He goes to his wife first, and they bid each other a fond farewell.

Bobby turns to his children. Tears flow freely. They are not ready to let go.

"Don't be sad," he says. "I will always be here looking after you, the people and the farm. This place has always been

Chapter 35 ~ Bittersweet

a refuge for me, and so it will be for you. Remember this, when you feel a tickle on your feet while you're sleeping, or a pat on the head when you're alone, it will be me looking in on you."

"I always knew that was you, Pappy," Mike says.

"Sammy and Patti, you have been given a gift. Use it well," Lolo says to his daughter and granddaughter.

Waiting for Bobby by a cluster of coconut trees are his parents and siblings. A man dressed in a European suit, stands a little apart from them — Lolo Ciano's brother, Pepe the hero.

And so they say good-bye to the ghosts of their family's history.

Before he leaves with Pepe and Bobby, Lolo Ciano waves to Sammy. "Child, if you need me, you always know where to find me. In your dreams."

Sammy waves and waves and then they are gone.

Sammy and her whole family lived happily. That is, until the next adventure.

The End

Glossary

abanico	Spanish for handheld fan
arbularyo	folk healer, herbalist
anting-anting	charms to ward off evil
ate	respectful term used to address an older sister, woman employer or older woman
aumakua	Hawaiian guardian spirit or family protector
bahay kubo	small native hut
balete tree	Banyan tree
banig	native handwoven mat used for sleeping, or decorative wall hanging
barangay	village
barong Tagalog	man's dress shirt made from the fibers of the pineapple plant
bawal	forbidden
bonjour	French for "Good day!"
bruha	witch
bunot	coconut husk used for cleaning floors
butiki	lizard
capiz	a large thin translucent shell
carabao	water buffalo
cherie	French for "dear one"
cucinero	cook
dim sum	Chinese light meal; usually steamed dough filled with meat, vegetables, seafood, etc.

[291]

duwende	dwarf. The *Duwende* from Philippine mythology is one who can cast spells to harm or help people depending how they treat the *Duwende*. Usually they have a territory called "*punso*," often a mound of dirt. When one passes in the vicinity of the "*punso*," one should ask permission from the duwende, as in "*Makikiraan po*" or "seeking passage with your permission."
	It is believed that harming the dwarf's home would cause grave consequences to the person. In Spanish, the spelling is *duende*, which means elf or house spirit.
engkanto	enchanted creature
fiesta	feast or celebration
hijo or *hija*	endearing term for daughter or son in Spanish
keiki	Hawaiian for "child"
kuya	respectful term used to address an older brother, male employer or an elderly person who is not a relative
lola and *lolo*	grandmother and grandfather, also used as a respectful term for an elderly person who is not a relative
mestiza or *mestizo*	daughter or son of an interracial marriage
manghuhula	fortune-teller
mano po	a term of respect when younger people take the hand of an older person or a godparent and touch it to their forehead
merienda	midmorning or late afternoon snack

nanay	mother
opo	a respectful term for "yes" when an addressing an older person
pamaypay	Tagalog for handheld fan
salamat	thank you
siesta	afternoon nap
Tagalog	language of the people from the Tagalog regions in the Philippines
tikbalang	a mythical creature having the body of an ordinary person but the feet of a horse
tilapia	a kind of fish
tita and *tito*	aunt and uncle
Voila!	French for "Behold!" or "There it is!"
yaya	nanny

Prologue

The Mandarin Mannequins of Chinatown

The Beginning
Something Dark,
Something Sinister

The first man she hated was her father.

When she was a little girl back in China, he sold her to the village shaman. Her mother didn't even fight for her. There were too many mouths to feed, and she was the only girl among five siblings. The boys would be useful later on, but food and clothing were wasted on her, as her father said.

"You are wasted space," her father lamented. "Ah, Bao Yu, if only you had been a boy. You are crafty and certainly more intelligent than your dense brothers!"

"Papa, I can help my stupid brothers do their chores and teach them how to earn a living. I swear I'm good at it," the girl said, fighting for her right to stay with her family with all the charms a 10-year-old girl could muster.

From the doorway of their hut, Bao Yu watched anxiously as her mother packed her meager belongings. She begged and pleaded with her parents, but they would not listen.

"You'll be better off with the old man. He can teach you chants and spells. Maybe one day you will take his place in the village," her mother said, not looking at her, afraid she might relent and beg her husband to keep her only daughter.

Tears welled up in the girl's eyes, hoping to touch her mother's heart, but the older woman turned away and walked into the kitchen.

Her father, along with her stupid brothers, dragged her kicking and screaming through the streets of the small village, dropped her off like a sack of rice on the front steps of the old shaman's house.

That's how Bao Yu learned early on that men were not in tune with women, that they're crude and oblivious. Men had no regard for the feelings, desires and emotions of the opposite sex. She held no respect for weak women either, she felt only contempt and disgust for females who think of nothing except fawning over their men.

She began her life of servitude, with no hope of escape. Another man she would learn to hate, though she did harbor a begrudging respect for his magic power, which she deeply coveted. She was mistreated and abused, made to sleep on the floor, washed and cooked for the shaman. Her life was harder even than that of a household servant who might have some niggling privileges. But in return, the old man taught her well.

Oh yes, she certainly learned a great deal from the shaman. Not only the traditional way of healing people and casting spells for a good harvest, but also the secrets and knowledge from the ancient book he so carefully guarded. Bao Yu figured out early on that the old man's source of power came from the book. Despite repeatedly having her ears boxed, she tolerated the shaman's method of teaching her to read and write.

Her fortunes changed when she blossomed into a beautiful, stunning young woman. The shaman, now a doddering old fool, became enchanted with her. He promised her the moon, if he could only conjure it. She settled for his knowledge and magical arts and access to the book. Her chores ceased immediately. A young girl was hired to do all the menial labor around the house.

She took over all the old man's duties. She collected and controlled all the payment for services performed for the villagers. Her former teacher was pitifully grateful for any attention she gave him. Bao Yu became well known and respected. She had it all — except for one thing. Despite their cruelty, she wanted to win her family's affection. She began to support them, hoping to buy their love.

Her greedy father and brothers happily took everything she offered, with no appreciation. They still took her for granted, and so did her mother, still their slave. The love she hoped she could have was never shown. Her lazy father and brothers only asked for more, sending her mother as the emissary.

Seething with rage, she gave them an ultimatum. Accept her back as the daughter and sister she was meant to be, or suffer the consequences. They laughed at her. She hatched her plan.

First, she cast a spell on her family. Bao Yu stood in front of their old mud house in an elegant red, yellow and blue silk gown, clapping her hands, dancing, skipping about like a beautiful bird, her long rope of black hair flying, shining in the sun.

"May you all wallow in dirt, may you eat food scraps for the rest of your lives," she said, sealing the spell with a wave of her hand. She could have done even worse, but deep inside her heart, a flicker of longing remained.

Next was the old shaman asleep in his bed, blissfully unaware. She silently crept to where he slept, and with a pair of scissors, cut off his main source of power. Then she carefully slipped the treasured book out from under the bed.

He might have become soft headed at his age, but he could still track her down if he put his mind to it. She placed the shaman's power in a small ivory case and put it in a burlap bag along with the book. Now she could transfer his power to herself, but that would take some time.

"Come, Mei Li! Pack your things. We are going some place where we can start over," she told her loyal servant.

"Where are we going mistress?" The servant asked fearfully, looking at the shaman who seemed to have shriveled up. His loose skin hung on his bones like a wrinkled curtain.

"We're going to a big city far away from this pig-stinking village. I will need time to perfect my skills, and you will be my assistant. You would like that, Mei Li?" It was more of a statement than a question. Bao Yu knew she would get no argument.

They traveled by darkness through swamps and forests. Sometimes they ventured out onto a highway and a passing truck picked them up, the driver hoping the pretty young woman would show some gratitude. No such luck.

But her powers were soon running dry. It took everything she could muster to cross the border undetected.

Exhausted, they walked the rest of the way, heads bowed to the ground, too weary to notice their surroundings. At last the two women came upon the Mai Po Marshes Nature Reserve, a bird sanctuary. It seemed an eternity. At least they could hide here. They laid down and immediately fell into a deep sleep, completely spent.

An urgent tapping on her shoulder woke Bao Yu from her fitful sleep. She sat up to find herself on a bed of reeds surrounded by mangroves, and a loud chorus of fluttering wings, the cries and call of cranes, egrets, terns and gulls. Where were they?

"Mistress! Please wake up. Look!" Still groggy from sleep, she looked to where Mei Li pointed.

Right before her lay her dream. She felt she could reach out and touch it. All the aches and pains were forgotten, replaced by rapid beating of her heart, joy and relief. She felt new power coursing through her veins. Any time now, she would be fully recharged and ready for action. Bao Yu was ecstatic.

Mei Li rushed from the safety of their hiding place to have a better look.

She hissed an order that stopped the servant girl in her tracks. "You stupid girl! Can't you see we are not alone? If we are discovered, I will make sure you never have one moment of peace, ever! Now get back here."

Mei Li crawled back to her mistress.

"Sit there quietly, and let me think of a plan to get us safely out of here. I am ravenous. Take out the last of our pitiful food. I promise you this is the last time we will eat this slop," she said, biting down hungrily on hard bread not fit for even the birds.

Two women tourists from a tour bus that had come to the nature preserve stumbled upon them. A few minutes later, the same two women appeared to emerge from the marshy reeds, patting their hair in place.

"Act normal, Mei Li. We don't want to draw any attention. This illusion will only last for a few hours. But by the time these two are discovered, we will have reached our destination. No one will ever find us there," she whispered to her companion.

Behind them in the reeds, two unconscious forms were sprawled out on the ground, dressed in very shabby clothes.

And soon it came about that Bao Yu, the girl from the mud hut who was born with nothing, the girl who had been thrown away by her parents, found the path that led to her transformation.

"I like the name on this identification book," she said, reading the women's passports. "From now on my name will be Lily, and yours will be Blossom," she said.

"Blossom? What a pretty name. Thank you, Mistress," Mei Li said timidly.

"Be quiet. We have to get on that bus before it leaves us behind," said Bao Yu — now Lily — dragging her maid toward the bus.

All the other passengers were seated. The tour guide looked at his watch impatiently as the women took the last seats.

"Ladies, please remember that we are on a schedule. I hope this does not happen again at the next stop," he said. He continued to rattle on about being considerate of others when suddenly Lily gave him a withering look.

Just like a man, she thought. Thinks he's so important, throwing his weight around.

Her look of hate froze him. He blanched, turned around, walked back to his seat at the front of the bus, and ordered the driver to take them to their next stop.

The lush green background and a white spiral of birds climbing in the sky was left behind as the bus drove away. Soon the scenery changed drastically from the nature reserve park to an eyesore of concrete buildings side by side on either side of the road.

She felt a tiny twinge of sadness, but quickly erased it from her mind. This was not the time to dwell on man's stupidity and lament the loss of the beauty of nature. She had things to do — many, many things to do in her life. Lily foresaw a bright and prosperous future. She knew she could achieve it with her knowledge and powerful magic, thanks partly to that shriveled old man she left behind.

Her daydreaming was interrupted by the tour guide's voice announcing that they were approaching their next stop, one of the many shopping malls cropping up in the new territories of Kowloon that border mainland China. He seemed to forget what happened and wished everyone a pleasant two hours of lunch and shopping.

"Mistress, look what I found," Mei Li whispered in her ear. "This Blossom woman has money in her bag. We could shop for a few things we're going to need in our new home."

"What did I tell you my name was?" Lily stared daggers at her servant. "You will not call me mistress. But you're right, let's use some of this money and buy a few things."

They piled out of the tour bus with the other passengers. The tour guide avoided looking at Lily.

Crowded souvenir shops, clothing stores, restaurants, just about anything to tempt a tourist were lined up, side by side, each vendor vying for the attention of passers-by, hawking merchandise, boasting of its superior quality.

Lily and Blossom went into a clothing store. The anxious shop owner greeted them with offers of discounts on any of the clothes on the racks, except for the mandarin-collared blouses and jackets behind the glass case. Those were hand made and prices for the lovely, soft material made from the best silk were not negotiable. "Well, except maybe for the discerning client interested in only the best," the owner said, eyeing the beautiful woman, he shooed Blossom out of the way.

"She's with me, she is my assistant. Blossom helps me with my shopping," Lily said, tossing her head so her long hair caught his eye.

"Yes, of course, of course," the owner said, impatiently grabbing Blossom and pulling her out of the way.

"I want to see your blouses," Lily said.

The owner went behind the glass case, and pulled out different designs and colors of the blouses wrapped in plastic. "Is there a particular color the lady would prefer?"

"You call this superior quality?" Lily asked, yanking a blouse from its wrapper. "My assistant here can do a better job."

PATRICIA LAUREL

"I will give it to the lady for a special price," the owner said hopefully. The sale was lost, but it didn't hurt to try.

Lily's face suddenly lit up, as if a light bulb had switched on. "Come, Blossom. There's nothing we need here. Hurry!"

Once outside, Blossom meekly said, "I thought the blouses were very pretty. The red one would have looked good on you. It brings out the sparkle in your eyes."

Lily was so excited, she blurted out some of her plans. "Blossom, we are going to be rich. I've just realized a way to make a living. Of course, it will take time. I will have to consult the old man's book and transfer all his power to me."

"How will you do that, ah, Lily," Blossom asked, trying to get used to calling her mistress by her new first name.

"I'm going to open a shop that specializes in mandarin collared blouses. They will be very special. The shop will be exclusive only to women and their daughters, absolutely no men will be allowed in the store. They will have to wait outside, while I fit their wives and daughters."

"But you don't know how to sew, Lily," Blossom said.

"Oh, don't I? I can do anything I want with the help of magic, you dolt! Now, let's go back in the shop and buy one of those inferior blouses. I need a sample."

After lunch and more shopping later, the two women headed back for the tour bus. The bus was locked. They had no choice but to wait. "If we go back to the shops, we might return too late. I don't want another episode with that tour guide. It might arouse suspiscion," Lily said, sitting down on a bench.

She heard a kitten meowing nearby. She looked around to see if the mother cat was somewhere close. I wonder if she knows her young is hungry? What was that? In an alley right by the bus stop, something tiny was barely moving, mewling underneath a pile of rags near a garbage bin. Lily wanted to ignore it, but curiosity is a hard habit to break. She stood up to investigate.

Lily bent over and uncovered the moving pile of filthy rags. She covered her mouth to stifle the gasp of surprise. Lying in the midst of the dirty trash was an infant girl, not more than a few days old.

The bitter sadness and resentment of her early life washed over her like a wave on the ocean. Emotions heaved within her, leaving her weak. Anger took over.

"Blossom, come here at once! Take one of the shopping bags with the clothes. Hurry, before the others get back!"

Blossom handed her the bag. "Oh my goodness! It's a baby," she cried out.

"Now that you've established that, don't stand there gawking. Hand me that," Lily said, yanking the silk mandarin blouse from Blossom's hand. She picked up the infant girl and wrapped the blouse gently around her.

"Now go and quickly find some milk. Hurry!" Lily said, with exasperation. Blossom was indeed loyal and faithful, but certainly not the most clever or astute. Ah, nothing to do about that now, she thought to herself.

"But you," she hissed at the tiny girl. "You I will train to be like me." Cooing to a baby was not her style. She'd seen mothers do that nonsense with their children, and found it distasteful.

"What will I call you?" She asked herself, just as Blossom arrived with the milk.

"What about Bao Yu?" Blossom said. "Give her your old name, Mistress, as a remembrance."

"Fool," Lily rebuked her. "What is there good to remember about my miserable girlhood?"

Blossom's face fell.

"Wait," Lily said, "maybe you're right. But I will call her Jade, the same name but different."

Blossom looked puzzled. "Jade is Bao Yu in English, Lily explained.

Blossom fed the infant who squirmed hungrily. Lily watched as her helper dipped her finger in milk over and over and placed it in Jade's little, pink mouth. The infant sucked on the finger greedily until she sighed and went to sleep.

Satisfied, Lily did her illusion trick. With a wave of her hand, tiny Jade became an ordinary shopping bag full of clothes. Just in time, the bus driver, gnawing on a toothpick, returned. A few minutes later, the tour guide with the rest of the passengers.

Lily and Blossom with little Jade between them, settled back in their seats and continued the ride to their new home.

Twelve years later, on the island of Hong Kong …

The pink-faced monk in his billowing, saffron robe glided down the crowded sidewalk with great serenity. He held a dignified, black, British umbrella above his shaven head. In a heaving sea of chaos, taxis flashing past, neon signs everywhere, clouds of bus exhaust, people hurrying scurrying, buying, selling, calling out. Everywhere the smeared grime and bustle of trade, the clatter, noise, haste and hustle of a great city.

The monk, who was on a pilgrimage, moved along slowly, patiently, as if he floated on his own little cloud. He wore tiny bells on his sandals to announce his presence, but no one could hear their trills amid the roar of the Hong Kong street.

He carried a canvas bag slung over one shoulder, containing candles, incense and a small, ivory state of Ganesh, the boy God with his elephant head, the remover of obstacles. Ganesh to protect him from destruction, to provide him with limitless compassion, to preserve the tranquility of his heart.

Blossom hurtled into him at full speed, tearing down the sidewalk as if she had been fired from the barrel of a gun.

He stumbled, dropped the umbrella, almost went sprawling, righted himself.

Blossom was so mortified that she started to cry. She clumsily scooped up the umbrella, bowed deeply, babbled apologies. "Oh, Sir," she said anxiously, "Oh righteous Sir ..."

The monk merely smiled at her, took the umbrella and made a sign of blessing.

Blossom ran on, galloping down the sidewalk, bumping into people, drawing angry looks, startled glances, curses in several dialects.

The poor woman, the monk said to himself, resuming his unhurried glide, what has made that soul so fearful, so void of peace?

Blossom darted into an alley lined with shops, stalls and beer stands, burst into the dress shop.

"Lily! Have you seen the newspaper? It's all over the news. Several women have disappeared in our neighborhood. One woman was seen with her daughter, but only the daughter surfaced later in a daze, and didn't know what happened." Blossom said breathlessly, rushing in the shop almost colliding with Lily.

"Be careful, you clumsy fool!" Lily said, balancing a mannequin in the store's display window. "Can't you see I'm busy?"

"It's not safe for us here. We have to think of Jade. The police are going door to door asking our neighbors if they have seen anything suspicious. They'll be here any minute now," Blossom said, nervously peering outside, She was still subservient, but years in Lily's company had taught her to speak her mind.

"Don't worry, it will be fine. We'll say we didn't see anything, and even if any these women came in the shop, they walked out of here safe and sound. Anybody around here can tell the police that," Lily said, confidently. "But you're probably right, Blossom. I think it would be safer for us to move to another place."

She signaled with a raised eyebrow for Blossom to be quiet as Jade entered the shop. "Why are you home early from school? It's not time for school to be let out yet," Lily said.

Jade was beaming, as any child would who had been given a holiday. She wore a blue sailor suit dress with a white collar. Jade was short for a 12-year-old, with a round face, a wide smile, and dark, merry eyes. Her thick, coal black hair was pulled back straight and tied off in a long pony tail.

"It's because of what's been happening with the women around here. We were told to go straight home, and be with our mothers," Jade said.

"That is the reason why we are going to move. This is not a safe place for a woman like me with a daughter," Lily said, patting Jade on the head. It was her way of greeting the child, the only way she knew how to show her affection.

She envied the natural closeness Blossom had with Jade, but it's something that didn't preoccupy her. She was

PATRICIA LAUREL

glad her assistant took over that responsibility. It was now Blossom that Jade went running to when she needed help with simple motherly things, but Lily took over, none too gentle, with the more important duties like homework, molding the child's personality and teaching her to trust no one, especially men. She had plans for her daughter.

Her daughter was at an age where boys started noticing her. Lily remembered her coming home one day from school and saying, "Mama, there's a boy in school that won't stop teasing me."

"And what did you do?" Lily asked.

"Well, I sort of like him, so I don't mind."

Lily blew up. She made Jade stay home from school until she drilled the importance of staying away from boys into her daughter's head. A few days later, she paid the boy a visit at school. He never teased Jade again, and avoided any contact with her.

"Where are we moving to? Kowloon?" Jade asked, interrupting her mother's thoughts.

"No, we are going to move to another country," Lily said, as she reached for a map of the Pacific region.

Lily opened the folded map, and spread it on the table, studying it intensely. "There. That is where we will go," she said, pointing her finger on the map of the Philippines. Lily had made up her mind. She set her sights on Binondo, Manila's Chinatown.

About the Author

Patricia Laurel was born and raised in San Pablo, Laguna. She was educated in Manila until the age of 16, when she left for Germany. She finished her education in Europe and the United States and has lived abroad since 1968. She has worked for the European edition of *Stars and Stripes* newspaper and the Associated Press. She is a board member of the ABS-CBN Foundation of North America. Laurel and her husband, John Windrow, live in Honolulu, Hawai'i. She is the great-granddaughter of Maria Rizal, sister of Dr. Jose Rizal.

J. Orosa Paraiso, the illustrator, is an artist and neurologist. He lives in San Pablo, Laguna, Philippines.

A portion of the proceeds from the sale of this book will be donated to ABS-CBN Foundation and the School of Love and Hope, a school for mentally handicapped children.

Only If You Can Find Me is the first volume of a trilogy. The second book, *The Mannequin Mandarins of Chinatown* is expected to be published in 2007. The title of the third book is *The Wiesbaden Wizard*.